CW00549703

NEVER WAR

STAR MAGE SAGA BOOK 9

J.J. GREEN

INFINITEBOOK

BOOKS OF THE STAR MAGE SAGA

1

Wet. Groggy. Cold.

Carina opened her eyes and immediately started shivering. She'd been through this same scenario countless times over the years, but the repeated experiences didn't make it any easier. She couldn't see a thing. A blurry veil shrouded her vision. Yet she knew what she was looking at: the inner wall of the Deep Sleep chamber she had stepped into three years previously— she hoped it was three years, and that nothing had gone wrong to shorten or prolong her time in stasis.

"How do you feel?"

Bryce.

She remembered he'd been scheduled to wake up a week before her. "I can't see a thing."

"I'll wipe your eyes."

She felt a soft cloth move over her eyelids. When she opened her eyes again she could make out his dark figure leaning over her.

He took her arm. "This way, ma'am. Your carriage awaits."

She chuckled as she climbed out of the chamber, his grip steadying her. He wrapped a blanket around her and she sat in the a-grav medic chair. Bryce would take her to sick bay for a checkup and then she would spend the next few days recovering. Her digestive system would start functioning again and her heart would become accustomed to beating at its normal rate, not the beat-per-hour of Deep Sleep. Stasis Dreams—wild, colorful escapades of her imagination, impossible scenarios, fantastical creatures, visions of people long dead—would fade from her memory. They were already slipping away. Providing she suffered no permanent after-effects, in less than a week she would be entirely back to normal, as if she hadn't spent years unconscious, leaping forward in time.

How different this was than her first experience of Deep Sleep, when the Regians had taken over the ship and put Lomang and Mezban in charge. Then, she'd been hauled from her chamber, freezing and slippery, by the giant, Pappu. And the Lotacryllans had killed Cadwallader in cold blood, before the man even had the chance to wake up.

She bowed her head.

Bryce put a hand on her shoulder. "Thinking about Cadwallader?"

She nodded.

He squeezed her shoulder.

It was the same every time. Whenever she woke from Deep Sleep she was reminded of the lieutenant-colonel's death, though it had happened decades ago and light years across the galaxy.

So many had died. Atoi, her long-time merc comrade, Jace, the wise, patient, kind mage who had helped her so much, Stevenson, the *Duchess*'s pilot and her port in the stormy sea of her youth, Viggo Justus, the honorable Lotacryllan, Calvaley, the former Sherrerr officer, Halliday, who had protected Darius with his own body during the glider crash on Magog, and Captain Speidel, who had been like a second father to her. There had been more deaths. More than she wanted to recall.

Had it been worth it?

Bryce hadn't said anything. He was probably waiting for her to come around fully before he gave her the news. The mind took time to adjust during the first days after Deep Sleep and facts would slip in and out of memory.

She would find out the news soon enough. Yet even if they'd

succeeded, on a deeper level her question had no answer. Cadwallader, Atoi, Stevenson, and Halliday had been Black Dogs who knew the risks of the lives they'd chosen. Viggo and Calvaley had been military men too. Jace had been a civilian, but he'd also been a mage, and the mage creed was that they helped each other, always.

Was her goal worth the sacrifice of those who had helped to achieve it? She didn't know the answer and never would, no matter what happened.

Fogginess invaded her thoughts and she slipped into a doze.

When she woke again she was in sick bay and people near her were talking.

"*Shhh!* Oh, look, you went and woke her up, just like I said you would."

"Sorry, Carina."

She smiled. Her brothers and sisters were standing around her bed. "It's all right, Ferne. No need to tell Darius off. It's good to see you all again. Is everyone okay?"

How time had changed them. During the periods they'd spent out of Deep Sleep on the long journey, everyone had aged. Tracking the passing birthdays during long-distance space travel was impossible, but Darius had grown to a young man, dashingly handsome and as sweet-tempered as ever, while Nahla was about twenty and very serious. Ferne and Oriana were in their mid-twenties. As they'd gone through puberty Ferne had shot up but Oriana had stayed the same height—a fact Ferne enjoyed reminding her about frequently. Parthenia had moved into her thirties and had grown to resemble their mother so much that sometimes the sight of her gave Carina pangs of grief.

"We're all fine," Parthenia said. "I was allowed out of bed this morning. How do you feel?"

"Good." Carina pushed herself upright. "I could almost say I'm getting used to Deep Sleep."

"Don't say that," Darius warned. "You'll jinx it and we'll have to do it again."

"No way," Oriana whined. "I'm never getting into one of those chambers again. It's like dying, and you never really know if you'll wake up."

Though the risk of dying was small it was one of the dangers of Deep Sleep. Sadly, one time they had lost a Black Dog. It was a big relief to know Bryce and her siblings had been successfully revived.

"So," she said, "is anyone going to tell me what's happening? Did we make it?"

Darius was about to say something but Parthenia interrupted him. "Before we answer that, we have something to show you. I'll just check with Clarkson that we can take you out."

The doctor grudgingly gave her permission. However, she stipulated that Carina was not to walk anywhere due to the danger of falling and hurting herself. The a-grav seat was employed once again to take her out of the bay and into an elevator.

"Where's Bryce?" she asked as they ascended.

Nahla replied, "He's with Hsiao, Jackson, and Van Hasty on the bridge. They're going over the scan data. It's *very* interesting."

Naturally, Nahla must have been examining the data too. She might have changed physically over the years but she had remained as inquisitive as ever, to the point of positively snooping.

"In what way is it interesting?"

"We can talk about that when you're back to normal," Parthenia replied. "What we're about to show you will be enough for today."

They were going to the uppermost deck of the *Bathsheba*, and Carina knew exactly what that meant. Excitement began to build in her stomach.

The elevator doors opened and, surrounded by her siblings, she maneuvered her chair down the passageway. They halted outside the doors to the Twilight Dome. How often had she been here, looking out at the starscape? So many events had taken place in the space beyond those doors.

They went inside.

The lights were out. The only illumination was the starlight shining in through the transparent roof.

Except stars were not the only things shining out in the velvety blackness of space. She moved to the center of the room and looked up.

"It's beautiful, isn't it?" Darius whispered.

Hsiao had positioned the ship so the object occupied the middle of the wide view.

A sapphire and emerald orb swathed in pearl-white clouds sat among the stars.

"Yes, it is," she breathed.

It was the most beautiful planet she'd ever seen.

Earth.

2

"Hey, Lin. You look like shit."

Van Hasty's greeting as Carina stepped onto the bridge made her smile. "You look worse. Did you spend the past five years awake?"

"Nah, I only feel like I did."

How old was the merc now? She had to be in her early forties. The long voyage had weighed heavily on the Black Dogs. The military men and women hadn't dealt well with years of inactivity. They thrived on action and risk, yet there had been little else to do since leaving their last port of call, Sot Loza, except spend time with other people—not their greatest strength.

Carina's family had fared better. They'd grown up, developed their self-identities, and honed their skills. They were ready for whatever new adventure awaited them on Earth.

"Don't pay any attention to her," said Hsiao. "You look great."

Carina slid into a seat at a console and opened the screen. "Where are Bryce and Jackson?"

"Checking for signs of damage."

"Did something happen while we were in Deep Sleep?" The chances of an asteroid strike were tiny but not non-existent.

"There aren't any reports but it doesn't hurt to get a visual."

She brought up the files of data pertaining to Earth. "So, what do we know?"

"A lot," the pilot replied. "Too much, almost. Have a look and you'll see what I mean."

The scan data *was* interesting, as Nahla had said. The most interesting thing about it was that it went back thousands of years. The *Bathsheba*'s scanners had been detecting attenuated, garbled comm signals light years before she arrived in Earth's system. The planet was *old*. She recalled a meeting with Jace and Cadwallader after the taking of the *Bathsheba*, where, with Jace's help, the lieutenant-colonel had calculated seven thousand years had passed since mages left Earth. The data completely fit in with his guess.

Seven thousand years since her ancestors had left the planet? It was an impossibly long time to imagine. Hundreds of generations of mages had lived and died, and she and her family were the first to return. What would they find?

The stories of the mages leaving told of pitched battles as the non-mages tried to force them to stay and fix the problems humanity had created for itself: a volatile climate, constant war, poverty and suffering for the vast majority of the population. But all the people could offer in return for the mages' help was persecution and servitude. They'd had no choice except to take advantage of the newly developed interstellar starship engines and depart, seeking worlds where they could live in freedom without fear.

And look how well that turned out.

"What do you think?" asked Hsiao. "What's the plan?"

"Stars, give me a minute."

There was no plan. Their actions depended upon what they found upon arrival, and what they'd found was almost too much information to digest.

As the *Bathsheba* had neared her ultimate destination, the data had become clearer and more recent, naturally. Over the long years, the ship's computer had done an excellent job of analyzing the language and translating it to Universal. Carina searched the media broadcasts, personal conversations, entertainment shows, company communications, and educational programs for mentions of mages.

There weren't many, but there were some. However, everything she read or heard pertained to the fabled image of her kind—mages were imaginary beings from fairy tales, something akin to witches and wizards. There was no mention of Casting except in relation to casting a spell. She saw nothing about the Characters, and the only references to elixir related to something called the Elixir of Youth.

It was all nonsense. Had humanity entirely forgotten about the real mages they'd driven away millennia ago? It seemed impossible. She felt she was missing a clue.

"Are you going to sit there all day?" Hsiao asked. "Decisions need to be made, Carina."

She straightened her back and stretched out her arms, noting with surprise she'd been going over the data for a couple of hours. Before she could answer, the bridge door opened and Bryce and Jackson walked in.

"Glad to see you're finally paying us a visit," said Jackson. "Your bed got uncomfortable?"

She rolled her eyes as Bryce leaned down for a kiss. "Everything shipshape?"

"The old girl's holding up well," Bryce said. "Just a few scratches still self-repairing on the hull."

"Did you run an armaments check?"

"Does Pamuk fart like a horse? All checked and ready for action."

"Let's hope it doesn't come to that." Her brief dive into the wealth of data about Earth indicated it wasn't steeped in military conflict. Aside from some minor, civil wars, the planet seemed relatively peaceful. Of course, information about defense capabilities wouldn't be available for cursory inspection.

"Come on, Carina," said Hsiao. "How are we going to do this? You've had the entire voyage to think about it."

"Introduce mages to Earth? That's going to take some thinking about."

"No, I mean where am I to park this ship? She isn't exactly petite or hard to notice. Anyone watching the skies will pick us up soon, if they haven't already."

"Ahh, I see what you mean. I'll ask Darius to Cloak us."

"Will that work?" Bryce asked.

"We'll try it," she replied. "He can't Cloak the *Bathsheba* indefinitely anyway. Someone's going to notice us eventually. We'll just have to deal with it when the time comes. Hsiao, I can see that Earth has a large, tidally locked moon. After Darius has Cast, take us to the far side. We can hide there while we figure things out."

"Got it."

Carina Sent to her youngest brother to make the request.

Now they'd finally arrived at their destination taking the next step felt hard. She'd been focused on getting here, fighting to overcome all the obstacles that had stood in their way. Their actual arrival in Earth's system seemed anti-climactic and the days ahead foggy and obscure. She'd wanted to find a place where mages could live in the open without fear. Then they might finally be able to use their powers for good, to improve the state of humanity. But how to get to that point was a mystery.

As if sensing her anxiety, Bryce said, "One step at a time."

She breathed deeply and exhaled. "Yeah, one step at a time."

OVER THE THOUSANDS of years that had passed following the mages' departure from their collapsing home planet, Earth's climate had stabilized, the cities had regrown, and technological development seemed to have resumed. The human population stood at three and a quarter billion—the largest of any world Carina had ever known. No single power or organization governed the planet as far as she could tell from the data. Even if there were a single entity to approach, she wasn't sure if that was wise.

As the *Bathsheba* hung in geostationary orbit on the far side of Earth's moon, she pondered the facts over and over, the weight of her predicament growing heavier and heavier day by day, until one day at the start of an active shift Darius came to see her in her cabin. Bryce had gone to breakfast and she was listening to the computer's translation of the latest broadcasts from Earth, trying to make sense of what she was hearing.

He leaned in at the open doorway and immediately her heart lifted. Though she loved all her brothers and sisters equally she shared a special bond with Darius, first forged when she'd rescued him as a frightened child, tortured by Dirksen thugs. He was tall now, taller than Bryce and Ferne, but to her he would always be that little boy who had entrusted an anonymous young merc with his life.

"Hey, Carina. I saw you weren't at breakfast."

"Not hungry. How are you doing? Come in and talk to me. I'm sick of listening to this nonsense from Earth."

He smiled at her invitation and sat next to her on the bed. "What nonsense is that?"

"Ugh, I don't know. It's a news channel, but I can't make head nor tail of who they're talking about or why. What have you been doing?"

"Well..." he paused and looked at her from under thick, dark brown bangs "...I've been waiting."

"Waiting for what? Oh, you mean..."

"Yeah. We're all waiting for you to—"

"Decide what happens next." She grimaced. It was embarrassing. In all the years it had taken them to journey to Earth, she'd had plenty of time to think through the possibilities of what they might find and come up with strategies to meet her goals, but now she was here she had nothing to suggest.

Darius said, "Maybe we should just go down there and see what happens. We could do that re...re... That thing the military does."

"Recon. Yeah." Reconnaissance would definitely be a good idea. There was only so much you could learn listening to broadcasts. In fact, lately she'd found the practice left her more confused than enlightened. Getting boots on the ground would reveal a whole lot more about human society on Earth and what mages might reasonably expect in terms of treatment.

Sending a team to the surface was the obvious move, but something held her back.

Darius asked softly, "Are you worried about what might happen?"

"Uhh..."

When her youngest brother asked questions like this, they were rhetorical. Though he couldn't read her thoughts—or at least he'd never admitted to being able to do it—it was no secret that he knew how she felt. He knew how everyone in his immediate proximity felt. As a Spirit Mage he couldn't help it. No one liked to mention his ability because it made everyone uncomfortable, including Darius, but they all knew it.

"I guess I am a little worried," she confessed. "So many people died to get us here," she continued, her voice catching in her throat. "What if it wasn't worth it? What if there's nothing for us on Earth? We've come so far, lived out so many years just flying through space. Most of your childhood has been spent on a starship..." Her words petered out.

Darius wrapped an arm around her shoulders. "And I couldn't wish for a better one. I've grown up among the people I love. What could be better than that? Do you think I would have had a better time living with my father?"

She sniffed. "Good point. I'll let you have that one."

"You know, I think Mother would be so proud of you. Look at everything you've done. You saved her children from the Sherrerrs, and you've done everything in your power to protect us, even to the extent of stealing a colony ship."

"It wasn't *exactly* stealing," she demurred, in an effort to lighten the mood. Their mother was never far from her thoughts.

He went on, "And you've brought us halfway across the galaxy to find us somewhere safe to live, somewhere we can be ourselves. Mother couldn't have asked any more from you, and neither do we. Neither does anyone on this ship. We all know the dangers, Carina, and if we didn't accept them we wouldn't be here. We're with you, come what may."

She was silent.

"So you're sending down an away team today?"

She swallowed. "Do I have a choice?"

"Maybe you can choose who's going to be in it."

"Thanks."

"To an extent."

3

The argument had been going on too long.

"Ferne and Oriana," Carina snapped, "you're staying here, and that's the end of it. There will be plenty more opportunities to visit Earth. Heck, hopefully one day you'll live there and you will have all the time in the world to explore, but for now we need mages aboard the ship."

"So let Parthenia and Darius stay," Oriana whined, pouting.

Carina had seen that pout many times over the years but familiarity didn't make it any less irritating. "Parthenia is the oldest and most experienced of all of you, and Darius is the best at Casting. That's why I've picked them and whether you agree with it or not, that's my decision."

"Leave it, sis," Ferne said irritably. "You won't change her mind. You know what she's like."

What I'm like?

Darius said, "I don't mind sitting this one out if it'll make things easier."

"It won't make anything easier," Carina replied. "You're coming."

"And I suppose Bryce is going too?" Oriana asked.

"Bryce is in the away team, yes. I suppose you don't like that either."

"Figures."

"Leave it, Oriana!" Ferne repeated.

"Nahla isn't coming either," Carina said. "She isn't complaining."

"Nahla's more interested in analyzing all the data from Earth," Oriana retorted.

Ferne tugged her sleeve. "Let's go and find something else to do."

"We've done everything there is to do around here," Oriana objected, "a thousand times over. I want to walk on grass again, feel the wind, and look up into a blue sky."

"And you will," Carina said, softening. Everyone on the *Bathsheba* felt the same. Though the ship was vast, living aboard it didn't compare to being planetside, and no one had been planetside in a very long time. "The next time the shuttle goes to Earth, you'll be on it. I promise."

Oriana turned and left the shuttle bay without saying another word. Ferne said, "She'll be all right soon enough. She's just bored. That's all."

"I know. I understand."

"Good luck, everyone." Ferne also left, passing Bryce as he entered the bay.

"What's up with Oriana?" Bryce asked. "She gave me her death glare in the passageway a minute ago."

Parthenia replied, "She's just being herself. Who are we waiting for, Carina?"

"Hsiao's flying us down. Jackson and Pamuk are on their way too. Van Hasty's going to keep an eye on things here while we're gone. I thought it was best to keep the team small. The more people we have the greater the risk of someone getting into trouble. When we have a better idea of what to expect we can increase the numbers."

"Do we have translators?" asked Parthenia.

"Oh, yeah. I was forgetting." Carina handed out the devices, which hung around the neck.

Bryce asked, "Do *they* have translators? Or are they going to think these are weird?"

"They do, but the ones I've seen in vids clip to the ear. I couldn't get the printers to fabricate them. These will do."

Bryce fingered his doubtfully. "What about clothes? Aren't we going to stick out?"

"We're going to stick out regardless. It will look more suspicious if we try to blend in and fail spectacularly. People will wonder what we're trying to hide."

"Right, so what's our story? You weren't planning on announcing we've just arrived from outer space, surely."

"I'll go over it on the way there."

Hsiao walked into the bay accompanied by Pamuk. The two looked comical next to each other. Pamuk dwarfed the petite pilot by half a meter and was brawny while Hsiao was slight. Carina was not a small woman herself, but the female mercs made her feel that way sometimes. She vividly recalled the burly merc simply lifting her out of the way when she tried to prevent her from leaving their residence on Sot Loza.

Pamuk was picking her teeth. "Jackson not here yet?"

"He's on his way," Carina replied, remembering Bryce's remark about her away team companion farting like a horse. She hadn't met many horses in her time but his observation was spot on. And she was about to share a cabin with her. Perhaps Van Hasty would have been a better choice. But there were few people she felt comfortable entrusting the *Bathsheba* to while they were gone.

Jackson arrived.

"We're all here," Carina said. "Let's go and take a peek at Earth."

"Hold on," said Jackson. "I've been checking the manifest. Thought you could use an update on supplies and so on."

"Good idea, but I'll take a look later. I've put off this trip long enough."

He continued, "I also wanted to make sure everyone was accounted for before we left. We're two people down."

She blinked. "That isn't possible. How could we have lost two people over the last leg of the voyage? I mean, even if the computer hadn't recorded something happening to them, they would have been missed by now."

"I've passed on the information to the medics. I guessed they must still be in Deep Sleep, and I've a good idea who they are."

"Who? Ohhh…" She cringed. She'd entirely forgotten the people in question too.

Bryce chuckled. "It's Chi-tang and Cheepy, right?"

"Bingo," Jackson said.

Their two 'pickups'—one from Lakshmi Station and the other from Sot Loza—had been nothing but trouble. Separately, they were bearable, Chi-tang more so than Cheepy. Chi-tang was their resident expert on the *Bathsheba*'s primary weapon, fondly nicknamed the Obliterator. In some ways he was quite smart, though not in the area of human relationships. Cheepy was a spoiled rich girl. As Chi-tang's first girlfriend, she'd made a split-second decision to accompany him to the ship before Carina had rained hell on her planet.

Despite the fact that her decision had probably been wise she'd regretted it, loudly and at great length, ever since being Transported to the *Bathsheba*'s bridge. She mostly blamed Chi-tang for her predicament and, after immediately breaking up with him, had hounded him with her complaints ever since.

The Black Dogs were seriously lacking in the compassion department. Although Cheepy's presence on the ship wasn't exactly Chi-tang's fault, the mercs blamed him for having an annoying ex-girlfriend. Consequently, the two had been sentenced to far longer periods of Deep Sleep than everyone else had to endure, and, it seemed, now the *Bathsheba* had reached her destination, no one had wanted to wake them.

Carina said, "The medics will get on it while we're gone. Chi-tang and Cheepy will be up and around soon."

"Awesome," Pamuk commented. "Something to look forward to when we get back."

DARIUS CLOAKED the shuttle all the way down, making them invisible to detection. Carina had picked a small town on one of the larger continents as their first experience of human society on Earth. The town's population was around 20,000. She hoped this meant it wouldn't possess the high-tech monitoring that city authorities used for security, yet it also wasn't a tiny, backwater place where newcomers would attract immediate attention.

Hsiao set down in a clearing in the forest that bordered the town. They had arrived in the early morning. The sun was just rising, and the shuttle's scanners told them no human-sized life forms were about for kilometers around, though the vessel's descent spooked some large specimens of local wildlife grazing in the open space. Perhaps the animals sensed by instinct that an object was approaching from above. Once the vessel was down they covered it in a camouflage blanket Carina had printed.

After they had hammered in the spikes that held the blanket in place, she took a few steps back to assess the results.

The blanket wasn't entirely effective viewed from the side. It worked by deflecting the light hitting it, guiding the waves around the object it covered. So at first glance the clearing looked empty but it was also faintly blurry or smudged. An aerial view was probably more convincing, and that was what really mattered. Satellites and passing aircraft would soon spot a starship shuttle that had appeared from nowhere, but the chances of hikers or hunters stumbling upon the shuttle were low.

"It's not too bad," Bryce commented.

"It'll have to do."

"Let's go meet some Earthlings," said Jackson.

They shouldered their packs, containing water and food supplies, and set off, leaving Hsiao to wait for them at the shuttle. They were unarmed. Earth seemed generally peaceful and civilized, and the last thing they wanted to do was to get into a firefight. In the event of a conflict they would walk away. The mages could Cast them out of trouble if things got dicey. The object was to not attract attention.

The forest was cool, humid, and quiet. Large ferns and small, thorny shrubs covered the ground between the trees. Carina had mentally debated the possibility of Transporting everyone closer to the town, but she didn't dare risk someone spotting them materializing out of thin air. Without a good knowledge of exactly where they would be Transporting to it was a real possibility.

There was no trail nearby. Forced to push through the undergrowth, they were soon dirty, sweaty, and scratched by thorns. If their unusual clothes didn't attract attention when they reached the town, their appearance surely would. It couldn't be helped.

They headed downhill, trying to seek out a water course. They didn't find one, but they did hit upon a path of sorts, leading through the trees and roughly in the right direction. They were nearing areas frequented by humans at last.

Darius kept lagging behind, and after calling a halt for the fifth or sixth time to allow him to catch up, Carina grew irritated. She told the others to wait for her and stomped back up the path to find her brother.

He was standing still, a hand resting on a tree trunk as he gazed upward at the canopy.

"Darius," she snapped. "What are you doing? You're slowing us down. We don't want to be walking back through these woods in the dead of night."

"We can Transport back to the shuttle," he said simply, his attention remaining on the tree.

"Well, yes, but..." she spluttered. "What *are* you doing?"

"It has feelings, you know."

"The tree?"

He gave her a 'what do you think I meant?' look, but only said, "They're faint, but I can feel them."

"Right." She regarded the tree. "How does it feel?"

"Calm, and..." he frowned "...content."

"I guess that's how a tree *would* feel. If you're done communing with the vegetation, it would be great if you could join us."

"Sure."

"That was a little mean. Sorry
."

"It's okay, sis."

They walked down the trail, Carina going in front. It occurred to her that Darius had spent more than half his life aboard a starship. This was his first experience of a natural environment in a very long time. She said over her shoulder, "If you want to do that kind of thing

—talking to the trees, I mean—I don't mind, but we're in a hurry today."

"I wasn't talking to it."

"Whatever you want to call it, it's fine, but—"

"I get it, Carina."

They caught up to the others and continued the trek. The woodland began to thin out. A place for eating picnics appeared ahead of them, ten or twelve wooden tables with benches dotted about and a children's climbing frame in the center. No one was here, however.

Then, beyond the trees, Carina spotted her first Earth dwelling. She pointed. "Look."

The habitation seemed to be *made* of earth too. Thick bricks of what looked like dried mud formed the walls of the single-story home. The roof overhung the walls, and it was alive. Living plants grew all over it. In some areas vines dangled all the way to the ground.

"Should we knock at the door?" asked Jackson. "Introduce ourselves as visitors from outer space?"

"Quit kidding around," Carina said.

It was mid-morning. The sun had risen above the trees and was shining through the open window shutters of the house. She couldn't spot anyone, which implied they also hadn't been spotted.

"I don't understand," Parthenia said. "I thought Earth was quite technologically developed. That house looks very simply constructed, and there are no power lines running to it."

Jackson replied, "You'll get many different levels of living standards on a planet. That place only represents one of them."

Bryce, who had walked away from the group to take a look from a different angle, asked, "Is that a well?"

"No electricity *or* running water," Parthenia commented.

"Let's head farther into town," Carina said.

They took a route that led them around the house and mostly out of sight of it. A wide dirt track ran down a slope from the forest and through low scrub. Beyond it was the town proper, though it was difficult to spot at first. The reason for this was the fact that the roofs of all the town's habitations were similarly covered in green plants, causing them to blend into the landscape. What gave it away was the regularity of the houses and roads laid out in a grid.

They saw their first people of Earth, riding bicycles or walking.

"Where are the cars?" asked Parthenia.

There were none.

"Well, one thing's for sure," said Jackson, "we aren't going to look weird for walking into town."

"Someone's coming," Bryce said.

Six people were approaching up the track. It was not a family group. They were all adults, and their clothes were similar. All wore dark blue slacks and a white top. Carina was confused. Were they wearing a uniform? There was sufficient variation in their clothing to imply it was not, but the similarities were too great to be random chance.

"What do we do?" Bryce asked. "Run? Fight?"

"Speak," Carina said. "We speak to them. This is a fact-finding mission, remember? We aren't doing anything wrong so whoever those people are they shouldn't be a threat. We stick to the story. We're from a remote island they probably never heard of, on vacation, just walking through the woods. I'll do the talking."

When the leading woman in the party arrived within speaking distance, she called out to them.

Carina's translator repeated the words in Universal: "Hello. Welcome to Earth. You're under arrest."

4

Carina ran.

Among the many conversations they'd had during the flight down, one thing they'd agreed was that if they were attacked, they were to split up and meet back at the shuttle. Hoping the others remembered the plan, she raced for the trees.

The police—or whoever those people were—didn't have weapons out, so she might reach cover before any of them got a shot off.

She thudded through the long grass, shouts of *Stop! Wait!* echoing in her ears. There was also the sound of a scuffle, as if someone had been caught. Guiltily, she hoped it was Jackson or Pamuk, who were used to being manhandled. Hell, after the interminable, boring voyage, they might even enjoy it.

The trees were only meters away.

She might make it.

"You!! a voice directly behind her called. "I order you to halt."

Oh, sure. Anything you say.

She reached the shade of the canopy. She'd nearly made it. Once she was in the forest she would be much harder to hit.

There was an explosive sound—not a detonation, but more like a discharge with force—something flashed across her vision, and suddenly her arms were pinned to her sides and her legs forced together. She fell, face forward, onto the dirt.

Pounding footsteps came to a stop next to her head. "You should have listened and done what you were told," the voice complained. "This is completely unnecessary."

Carina's cheek pressed into the prickly woodland floor and her hair had flopped over her eyes. All she could see was empty nut shells from the tree and the boots of her captor. Her limbs were tightly pinioned. She guessed her assailant had fired some kind of entrapping device. Her arms and legs felt as though they were tightly wrapped. Perhaps what she'd seen had been the cords or ribbons flying around her body.

"Wait here," the voice said. "I'll be back for you in a minute."

Like I have a choice about it.

Over the years, as Bryce and she had grown into the familiarity of a long-married couple, though, technically, they weren't married, he'd grown sufficiently comfortable to tease her about her magehood. Whenever she screwed up, such as by programming the printer incorrectly and creating a disgusting dinner, he would say something like *Being magic didn't make you a great cook, did it*? Or if they were doing target practice and he beat her, he would patronizingly comment, *Never mind. One day you'll learn how to Cast a great shot.*

That was the thing with non-mages. They imagined being able to Cast was some kind of cure-all, a fix for each and every situation. But there were so many limitations they didn't take into account. Here on Earth, she couldn't risk Casting in front of the natives. The whole point of being here was to find somewhere safe for her and her family. They couldn't reveal their secret without risking the beginning of the whole slavery-and-torture cycle that mages in distant parts of the galaxy devoted their lives to avoiding.

But even if she could openly Cast here, how could she possibly drink elixir, create the Transport character in her mind, send it out, and wait for it to take effect, in the time available before she was captured? Running away was the faster, more effective, and pragmatic solution.

Not that it had worked this time around.

The boots returned. "Right. Let's get you on your feet." A hand grasped the back of her shirt and helped her stand upright.

She was staring into the face of a sandy-haired, hazel-eyed young man, roughly mid-twenties. Like the other Earth men, his hair reached his shoulders and he was clean-shaven. Most of the men on the *Bathsheba* had given up on shaving regularly. Even Bryce had a short beard.

"Where are my companions?" she asked, peering over his shoulder. She caught a glimpse of a group being led away, but only heads and shoulders were visible as they descended the slope.

She looked down. Her body from her chest to her knees was encased in thin, transparent threads.

"Is that a translator around your neck?" The man leaned closer. "If I free your legs, do you promise not to run? There's no point. I'll just catch you again with this." He gestured at a box on his belt. "It won't be fun to plant your face in the dirt again, will it? You might get hurt."

He reached toward her face. She flinched and pulled back.

"Take it easy." He brushed her cheek and nut shells that had embedded in her skin dropped to the ground.

For a law enforcement operative, he was being excessively polite.

"I'm not promising anything," she retorted. "Let me go. You've got no right to hold me captive. I haven't done anything wrong."

His eyebrows lifted. "That translator is so cool. I've never seen one like that before. I'd love to take a closer look at it but we really need to go now. I'm going to free your legs. Please don't run. I'd rather not hurt you."

He took a short knife from a sheath in his belt and slit the threads enveloping her thighs. "It's only a short walk to the station. You go in front, where I can keep an eye on you."

She might have been able to get away from him. She could have kneed him in the balls and fled into the forest. But there was no way she would be able to cut the threads around her torso by herself, and it was a long trek back to Hsiao at the shuttle. She also had no idea where the captured members of her party were being taken, and she clearly stuck out as a stranger. Somehow, the man knew she wasn't even from Earth. Rescuing her companions could be impossible in the circumstances.

She stepped in the direction of the trail.

"Glad you're finally seeing sense," the man said as he followed her. After a few more steps, he added, "So, where are you from?"

"What makes you think I'm not from Earth?"

"Huh? Oh, you mean what the sergeant said." He chuckled. "You don't speak English, so I guess she must be right."

The situation was becoming more and more bizarre. English had to be the name of their language.

"So what if I don't speak English?" she said.

He chuckled again. "Most people speak English. Except you and your friends, that is. I mean, I'm not saying there's anything wrong with it, but you can't deny it. You must be from offplanet."

They had walked down the slope, giving her a better view of the group ahead. Darius, Parthenia, and Bryce had been caught. Pamuk and Jackson must have got away and would be heading back to the shuttle.

"I know what you're thinking," the man said. "You're thinking we didn't catch all of you. But we will. It's only a matter of time."

"Where are you taking us?"

"You'll wait in the lockup until the magistrate arrives. He has the final decision on what to do with you, but you'll probably go to the central court in Bridgeford. After that, who knows? The capital, I suppose."

"But we haven't done anything wrong," Carina protested.

"You're illegal aliens, from outer space of all places! I'm sorry, ma'am. I didn't write the laws, but it's my job to enforce them."

"How did you know we were here?"

"Sensors in the woods, of course."

"They detect people? Aren't people allowed to wander around in there?"

"Absolutely. I go up there all the time with my friends. But you triggered them."

"How?"

"Like I said, you're illegal. Set off the alarms."

"But how?"

"You'll have to ask a technician. I don't know how they work. How did you end up in the forest?"

She didn't answer. As they drew near the group in front, Parthenia looked back and her face fell. She must have been thinking her eldest sister had escaped and might help her, Darius, and Bryce out of their predicament. Carina gave her an apologetic smile.

They caught up to the group and Darius also noticed her. "Oh, no. Not you too."

"Don't worry. Everything's going to be fine."

Bryce smirked.

They were escorted into town. It was an odd place. For a human habitation it was remarkably alive. The roadways—or perhaps it was better to describe them as pathways as no motorized vehicles ran on them—were paved, but everywhere else was green and growing. Grass surrounded each building, but it couldn't be described as lawn. The blades grew fifteen centimeters tall and other low-growing plants dotted the sward, some in flower. Shorter plants covered the roofs. Even the walls were growing surfaces, holding pockets of trailing vines.

Carina asked her affable law enforcement officer, "Why is everything so green?"

"What do you mean?"

"There's vegetation everywhere."

He frowned. "Why wouldn't there be?"

They passed through the open doorway of an official-looking building. A sign in English hung over the portal, but naturally she couldn't read it.

A woman in blue and white sitting behind a desk rose to her feet as they entered. "The aliens! Well, isn't this something? What are those things?" she asked, pointing. "Wait, I understand." She marched over and lifted Carina's translator to her lips. "What's your name?" The device converted her words to Universal. Without waiting for a reply, she laughed. "I love it." She stared Carina in the face. "Say something."

"Uhhh…"

The translator didn't repeat the utterance, and the woman's features expressed her disappointment. "Does it only work one way?" she asked Carina's captor.

"No, it works both ways. We had a little conversation, right?" He turned to Carina for confirmation. "Go on, say something for the sergeant."

In a tone of amazement, she asked, "This is your *superior*?"

When her translator conveyed her words in English, the sergeant's eyes grew hard, and she gave a cough before straightening her jacket. "Put them in the cells. I've notified the magistrate and he'll be here shortly."

As Carina and her companions were led away, the sergeant said, mockingly, "Take me to your leader." Then she burst into fits of laughter.

5

There were only two cells, and one was already occupied. A man in ragged clothing lay on his back on the bunk, snoring loudly.

"You don't mind all squeezing in together?" the officer asked, "only I don't want to wake Brian up. "You'll be cozy."

Carina stared at him while he ushered them into the cell. He cut the threads binding their upper halves, stepped out, and closed the door. She tried it, wondering if the kindness of their captors extended to not actually locking them in. It didn't open—probably magnetically sealed.

"You have to admit," Bryce commented, "for local law enforcement, they're pretty nice."

"Nice enough to imprison us," she muttered.

Darius sat down on the bunk, which was suspended from the wall on chains. "So...do we Transport?"

"Shhh!" She scanned the ceiling, walls, and floor, and bent down to look under the bunk. Though she didn't find any security devices, she remained unconvinced they weren't being monitored. Pretending to take a sip of water because she was thirsty, she swigged elixir, and then Sent to Darius and Parthenia: *No Casting. We don't know who's watching or listening, and we definitely don't want anyone to guess we need our elixir. They'll know all they have to do to control us is to take it away. We use Transport to escape only as a last resort.*

Her brother and sister signaled their understanding with their eyes, and Bryce clearly knew what had passed between them. He'd been a member of the family so long, little needed to be explained to him.

Their incarceration almost immediately after setting foot on the planet was definitely a setback, but it wasn't necessarily a disaster. For one thing, the authorities didn't seem to know where the shuttle was. If things got dangerous, they could get back to it. Pamuk and Jackson were probably already on their way there. In the meantime, the fact-finding mission could continue, though somewhat more restricted than she would have liked. She had already learned a lot. Earth natives seemed to be obsessed with natural environments, to the extent they grew plants everywhere they could squeeze them in. And their police service was remarkably friendly and casual. Nothing made much sense but maybe things would become clearer later.

She said, "Let's wait for the magistrate the sergeant mentioned. Maybe we can find out from him or her exactly what we're supposed to have done wrong."

The cells were down the corridor from the station entrance. She pressed her face against the transparent wall, angling for a look at what was going on. The wall that separated the cells area from the rest of the station was transparent too, but she didn't see much except a couple of police officers passing to and fro.

"Sit down," Bryce said. "We've been walking all morning. You must be tired."

"I'm fine."

Parthenia snapped, "You don't have to be on guard all the time, Carina."

She ignored her. The years they'd spent on the *Bathsheba* might have dulled her siblings' sensitivity to the dangers mages faced, but they hadn't dulled hers. She also had a sense of desperation that wouldn't allow her to relax her vigilance. If her family was to ever find a safe place to live, this was their last shot. She couldn't screw up.

Activity in the reception area increased. Several officers ran to the door, and there was a struggle as someone was brought in. Shouts and exclamations resounded dully through the barrier.

Darius got up and joined her. "What's that? Is something going on?"

"They've caught someone else, I think."

"Who?"

"I can't see. I only got a glimpse."

"Is it one of the mercs?"

"Maybe. Whoever it is, they're putting up a hell of a fight."

As they'd been talking, the sound of furniture banging about joined the noises of the altercation. Frustrated by her inadequate view, Carina pushed her face harder into the wall. Naturally, it didn't make any difference.

Three figures approached, the central person being held and dragged by the other two.

"It's Jackson."

Judging by the blood trickling from his scalp, the merc had been subdued by a blow to the head. He seemed barely conscious as he was forced to walk the distance to their cell.

"Stand back," one of the officers ordered. It was the man who had captured Carina. His affable demeanor had disappeared. He was pale and looked shocked. She guessed most of his prisoners were more compliant than a Black Dog who hadn't been in a fight for too long.

As they crowded into the far side of the cell, Jackson was brought in.

"He is one of your companions, right?" the officer asked. "Only, he's very dangerous." With the help of his colleague, he laid Jackson down on the bunk.

"Yes," Carina replied. "He's our friend."

"A friend? You should know, he killed someone. But he won't hurt you, I suppose?"

"No, he definitely won't."

The officer seemed relieved. He nodded to his fellow and they left the cell. With the door closed, he continued, "The doctor is on her way to take a look at him. If he comes around and turns violent, give a shout. The cells are monitored. Someone will definitely hear you."

So there *were* hidden surveillance devices.

As soon as the officers had left, Jackson swung his legs over the edge of the bunk and sat up, ruefully rubbing the back of his head.

"You shot one of them?" Bryce asked.

"Had to." He surreptitiously touched his prosthetic forearm, which concealed a weapon. "Didn't help in the end, obviously. That stuff that wraps around you is really effective."

The officers who had finally caught him must have thought he'd thrown his gun away. Someone was probably searching for it in the woods even now.

"They seemed astonished," Parthenia said.

"More like appalled," said Carina. "I get the impression this is a very peaceful society." It boded well for her aims, but if she was right Jackson was in a lot of trouble. They'd all become used to violence and death, moving on from one battle or conflict to the next. What were the repercussions somewhere these things weren't commonplace?

Parthenia dabbed at his wound with the hem of her shirt. "I would help, but..." She glanced at Carina.

"Don't worry," the merc growled. "I get it."

"Where's...?"

Jackson shrugged. So Pamuk, at least, had escaped. The monitors the officer had mentioned couldn't be placed throughout the whole forest or she would have been picked up. It was a shame neither she nor Hsiao were mages and couldn't receive Sent messages.

The man in the cell opposite stirred, moving his legs weakly. He turned onto his side and promptly fell off his bunk, hitting the hard floor with a thud that made it through two walls. While he was staggering upright, the officer returned.

"Now then, Brian. Take it easy. Get back into bed." He leaned nonchalantly on the wall, peering at the inmate without particular concern.

"Wanna go home," Brian slurred.

"You're not ready yet. Get some more sleep."

"I wanna go home." He thrust his hands into his pants pockets and rested his chest on the barrier. "The missus will be wondering where I am. Give me the shot and I'll be on my way."

To be fair, Brian did appear to be sobering up by the second.

"You know the law. Drunk and disorderly gets you twelve hours' jail time, for your own safety as much as everyone else's. You've only been here seven hours. You've got five hours to go."

"Come on, Matt. Give me the shot and no one will be any the wiser. I need to get home to the missus."

"You can comm her."

"If I comm her she'll know where I am."

It seemed an odd comment. Maybe comms were easily traceable here.

"Have a word with Betty," Brian went on. "Go on. Do a man a favor."

"Oh, all right."

"That's what I like to hear."

As the officer left to 'have a word with Betty', Brian noticed his fellow inmates. He stared, his bleary eyes sharpening their focus while his jaw slowly dropped.

Darius gave him a small wave.

He pulled a hand out of his pocket and waved back, his mouth continuing to hang open.

The sergeant—Betty?—appeared. She cast a dark look at Jackson before turning to the opposite cell. "Matt tells me you're agitating to leave, Brian. You know that's against the rules. What'll happen if it gets out that I let you go before your time was up?"

"But it won't get out. I won't tell a soul, I promise."

"Hmm... You'll give me your word?"

"Cross my heart and hope to die."

"And you'll attend the recovery course we booked you onto?"

"I'm looking forward to it. I've been wanting to turn over a new leaf for a long time."

"Okay, you can have your shot, but if I see you back here again you'll have to serve twenty-four hours. Do you understand?"

"Clear as crystal, Betty."

But before the sergeant could follow through with their agreement, she was called back into the reception area.

Her expression was grave when she returned. A man in late middle age walked behind her. Ignoring Brian, who watched with interest, Sergeant Betty said, "Here they are. They're all yours. Good luck with them." Gesturing at Jackson, she added, "That one's the murderer."

6

The handcuffs were made from a similar material to the cords the officers used to bring down suspects who were running away, except they locked. Officer Matt snapped the transparent bracelets around Carina's wrists.

"You're armed now," she commented.

He was carrying a handgun in a shoulder holster. "Uh-huh." He didn't look at her as he moved to Parthenia to put on her handcuffs.

Another officer—a beefy guy they hadn't seen before—had apparently been assigned to Jackson, who was hobbled as well as handcuffed. His wrists were behind his back too, while the other prisoners' hands were secured in front of their bodies.

"Why are you armed?" Carina persisted. "You weren't before."

Matt nodded at Jackson. "Courtesy of your friend here. The *murderer*," he added, shaking his head.

"I take it you don't see a lot of dangerous criminals."

He didn't answer her. His attitude toward her and her companions had changed. The friendliness was entirely gone and he wouldn't even make eye contact. The magistrate waited outside the cell with Betty, watching the prisoners being prepared for transfer. They were to go somewhere for a preliminary hearing. No one had explained any more than that.

"What did they do?" a voice called out.

Brian's release had been delayed by the magistrate's arrival, and he remained in his cell. He was craning his neck, trying to see around Betty. "Who are they? Did one of them kill someone?"

"Be quiet," said Betty over her shoulder, "or I'll make you wait for that shot."

"I was only asking!" Brian protested.

Two more officers waited with the magistrate and Sergeant Betty. With Jackson's minder and Matt, that made four. Despite the fact they were transporting a *murderer* the authorities still hadn't thought it necessary for their officers to outnumber the criminals.

They were led from the cell in single file, Matt in front. The man assigned to Jackson walked beside him, and the remaining officers brought up the rear. They took them out of the station. A crowd had gathered. Word appeared to have gotten out that some unusual criminals had been taken into custody. The people seemed to be local townsfolk, and they gawped in the usual way, obviously enjoying the fact they had something new and interesting to gossip about.

Bryce commented, "We're famous."

"But not in a good way," said Carina.

Parthenia muttered, "So much for remaining inconspicuous while we investigate Earth society."

Carina had expected to see a vehicle awaiting them, but there was only the crowd, which had spilled onto the road. Bicyclists were being forced to dismount to navigate a passage.

"Break it up," Matt ordered. "Nothing to see here. Move along, please!"

The people ignored him.

He tutted, elbowing a particularly nosy man aside as he forced his way through the throng.

"Stand back!" Jackson's guard commanded. He had greater success. The onlookers shuffled backward a few steps, murmuring and pulling faces.

"Where are we going?" Carina asked Officer Matt's back.

"Where do you think?" he snapped, without turning.

"How would I know? I'm new around here, remember?"

"Bridgeford."

The crowd followed them down the street, attracting new members.

"Why don't we go by car?"

He threw her an annoyed look. "We *are* going by car."

A cry like that of a warrior going into battle came from somewhere beyond the crowd. The people surged, pushed forward by those behind them. Some stumbled into the prisoners. Jackson's minder yelled and shoved at them, warning them to move back.

"What's going on?" Bryce asked.

Jackson said, "I think I recognized that—"

A burly figure pelted through a gap and crashed into Matt, shoulder to shoulder, felling him like a bowling pin.

Pamuk.

"I got you!" she hollered. "Carina! Bryce! Everyone, this way!"

Carina was frozen with shock. They were surrounded on every side, and the officers escorting them were armed, and Jackson was hobbled. Where did Pamuk think they were going?

The prisoners looked at each other uncomfortably.

"Come on!" Pamuk rammed the nearest people. "Get out of the way. Come on, guys!"

Carina half-heartedly followed her into the passage she was forcing, more out of sympathy and solidarity than any hope of escaping. Bryce came with her, his face a picture of secondhand embarrassment.

Jackson's guard pushed past them and laid a heavy hand on Pamuk, spinning her around. She threw a fist, smacking into his jaw. He staggered and drew his weapon. The crowd tried to move out of the way, tripping and falling into each other.

Carina jumped on his back, lifting her handcuffed wrists over his head and wrapping her legs around his waist. "Pamuk! Run!"

Hands clutched her, trying to rip her off the guard.

Pamuk grabbed at the gun, tugging hard. The guard fell forward, and everyone went down. Whoever had been holding onto Carina landed on top of her. She could feel the burly guard underneath her,

arching his back as he tried to get up. Where was Pamuk? She had to
be on the bottom of the pile.

What if the guard fired? Pamuk could be killed. And if she wasn't
killed right away she would be injured and the mages would have to
Heal her in front of everyone or let her die.

"We surrender!" Carina yelled, her face pressed into the guard.
"Don't shoot!"

"I don't surrender!" Pamuk's voice was muffled but her words were
clear.

"Yes, you do!"

"No way. Get off me you great lummox!"

"She doesn't mean it."

"Yes, I do."

The pressure on Carina's back lifted and she could breathe again.
Hands fastened around her waist and hauled her to her feet. The guard
managed to climb to his feet. As he did so, Pamuk appeared to finally
realize the hopelessness of the situation. She leapt up and turned to
run. But Officer Matt—the person who had picked Carina up—was
already reaching for his belt, though not his gun she was relieved to see.

The crowd had scattered. Matt had a clear shot, and Carina had
her first clear view of the device that had been used to bring her down
out in the forest. Long, liquid lines spurted from the black box,
gaining solidity in the air as they went. The ends touched the fleeing
Pamuk and then the rest of the lines whirled around her, wrapping
her up like a spider wrapping a fly.

She toppled to the ground. But even that didn't stop her from
trying to get away. She wriggled on her stomach, inching forward.

The other officers had corralled Parthenia, Darius, Bryce, and
Jackson together and were holding them under threat of being shot.
Matt rubbed a bruise on his head that must have been sustained
when he fell.

Jackson's guard dealt with Pamuk. He walked over to her and put
one boot on her back. "Where do you think *you're* going?"

The merc cursed. She was so loud and vile Carina was silently
thankful Darius was just about a grown man. The guard fiddled at his

belt and brought out a pair of handcuffs and a small knife. Slitting the threads nearest Pamuk's hands, he freed them sufficiently to draw her wrists together behind her and fasten the cuffs around them. Then he cut through the remaining threads, grasped her shirt at the neck, and jerked her to her feet.

"Thanks a lot," she said sarcastically. The remark was addressed at Carina.

"Hey, I was the one trying to save you from being shot."

"I was the one saving *you* guys! Why didn't you run when I told you?"

"Because how in all the hells would we ever have got away?!"

The guard barked, "Shut it. Both of you. Matt, you watch this one and her, right?" He meant Pamuk and Carina. "I'll take the murder suspect. Let's go while we have space to move."

The bystanders were regaining their confidence and approaching again.

The situation was bizarre. Why were they walking along a street, out in the open? In her time as a merc and even afterward, on all the worlds she'd visited, she'd never encountered such lax security. Perhaps Pamuk's idea that she might be able to free them wasn't so insane. If she'd been armed and had a vehicle, she might have done it.

"So where is this car you're taking us to?" Carina asked Matt as they continued.

He didn't answer her only snapped at the people in his way. Considering he was an armed police officer, they seemed surprisingly unafraid.

They approached a wide, open entrance. Tape had been strung across it at waist level, and the other side was empty. Matt halted and lifted the tape, telling Carina to go under it. When everyone in their group was on the other side, he warned the crowd that anyone who attempted to follow would be placed under arrest. Some of them seemed tempted, nonetheless.

They stepped onto an escalator that descended to a lower level.

"Hey," Carina said.

Matt, who stood on the step below her, didn't turn around.

"Hey." She poked him with a finger.

"Carina," Bryce warned.

"Don't worry. He's a nice guy. I can tell."

Bryce rolled his eyes.

"Officer Matt, I thought you said we were going by car."

"We are. That's enough questions."

The escalator ended at an open, tiled space. Carina got the impression it was a public space, but that the public were being excluded for the moment. They followed Matt under one of several archways and halted. They were standing on a station platform.

"We're going by *train*?"

"How else would we go?" Matt asked in return. "Here comes our car now."

A railway car sped toward them, borne along on the single rail track.

7

"Let me get something clear," Carina said, "you don't have vehicles that run on roads on the surface?"

They had the carriage to themselves. Long lines of seating ran down each side. It seemed to be a regular model for public use that the police had commandeered for transporting the prisoners. Matt sat between Carina and Pamuk, Jackson's minder sat next to him at the far end of the car, and the two remaining officers flanked Darius, Bryce, and Parthenia.

"I said," Matt replied testily, "that's enough questions."

"But we're from offplanet, remember? How do you expect us to learn about Earth if you won't tell us anything?"

"Not that again. Be quiet."

Pamuk's nose was bloody from where she'd hit it on the ground. As she wiped it on her sleeve, Matt glanced at her, and then fished in the top pocket of his jacket. He pulled out a tissue and dabbed at the blood.

Pamuk's eyes grew wide and her mouth fell open.

Matt folded the tissue in half and dabbed some more with the clean section.

"Wh-what the stars are you doing?" the merc stuttered.

Carina chuckled. There was nothing that could alarm a Black Dog faster than someone being nice to them.

"Seeing to the welfare of my prisoners," Matt muttered. "What do you think?"

Pamuk stared at Carina as if to check she wasn't imagining things.

Across the carriage, Jackson guffawed.

"Quieten down!" snapped his guard.

Jackson stifled his mirth. Matt put the tissue away, and Pamuk relaxed. Lights in the tunnel sped past. There was little sound, only the rush of air as they sped along the tunnel.

"How far is it to Bridgeford?" Carina asked.

Matt replied, "We'll be there in a few minutes."

"So, not far. Does everyone get around like this?"

He heaved a sigh. "Yes, everyone gets around like this. You're trying to tell me it's different where you're from?"

"What about freight transports?" said Jackson's guard. "Maybe that's what she means."

"Oh, the overground system. You mean going by freeway?"

"I don't know," Carina replied. "Do I?"

Matt said, "Heavy loads of freight are sometimes transported on freeways. The network is a little more extensive than rail."

"But what about people? Don't people travel by road?"

"I suppose people could go that way too, hitching a ride. But I don't know why anyone would."

"Can't they travel by themselves?"

"How would they do that?"

"In cars."

"But we're in a—"

"Not this kind of car. One that goes on roads."

"I don't know what you're talking about. I think we must do things differently on *Earth*. Where are you from, by the way?"

In some ways, it was a hard question to answer. "You wouldn't have heard of it."

"Maybe not, but it must have a name."

She told him the name of the impoverished, backwater planet where she'd grown up, two galactic sectors and a lifetime away.

"You're right," said Matt. "Never heard of it."

AT THE BRIDGEFORD STOP—THE train ran straight through several intervening stations—the immediate area had been made off-limits to the public. The news of their arrival must have traveled ahead. A crowd pushed against a temporary barrier erected around the station exit.

"Do criminal suspects usually receive this kind of attention?" Carina asked Matt.

"The interest is all on account of your friend there." He jerked his chin at Jackson.

"So there aren't many murder cases?"

"First local one I've heard of. I don't think there were any in my parents' time either."

Pamuk whistled. "You guys live in a fairy tale."

"Is it like that all over?" asked Carina.

"People generally don't go around killing each other. Is that what it's like where you're from? What a horrible place."

Carina began to worry about what might happen to Jackson, given that his crime was so rare. Judging from the expression on the man's face, he was worrying about it too. Killing a pursuer was a reflex action for a merc. She'd lost count of how many people she'd killed in her days with the Black Dogs. She'd killed a fair few subsequently too.

Did the crime carry a death sentence? If the worse came to the worst she would Transport Jackson to safety, regardless of whether that entailed revealing her powers.

At the edge of the cordoned-off section stood four armed men and women, wearing uniforms the same as Matt's. He made the prisoners wait at the station exit while he talked to them. When he returned his expression was glum.

"Sad to say goodbye?" Carina asked.

"I've been seconded to the NPS—National Police Service—apparently, for an open-ended period, due to my 'familiarity' with the prisoners." He huffed disconsolately. When his colleague, Jackson's guard, laughed, he added, "So have you."

The man's face fell.

"You two can go back," Matt said to the officers guarding Bryce, Darius, and Parthenia. "This way." He gestured for everyone to follow him.

The Bridgeford Police Force appeared to be more respected than the one in Matt's town. The crowd stayed back as they walked to the detention center. However, the town itself didn't seem very much different from the place they'd just left. Carina guessed they had to be in the central district, but none of the buildings were taller than two stories, and they were all verdant, with green roofs and trailing plants dangling down the walls. Some vehicles passed by that were larger than the bicycles they'd seen in the other place—covered three- and four-seaters and some pulling trailers—but all were pedal-powered.

"I like it here," Darius commented to Carina. "Don't you?"

"To be honest, I'm still trying to wrap my head around the place."

Parthenia said, "Darius, only you could be literally wearing hand-cuffs and on your way to a place of incarceration to await an unknown fate, yet still see the positive side."

"I quite like it too," said Bryce, glancing around. "The air's clean and I like seeing plants everywhere. It feels like we're in the country-side even downtown."

"I suppose it *is* nice," said Carina, "but it's also weird. You're forget-ting the sensors in the woods. What kind of government monitors their citizens to *that* extent? You can't even go for a picnic without the authorities knowing about it? I wouldn't like to live like that, with zero privacy."

Matt had overheard her. He said over his shoulder, "Those sensors are there to track kids who wander away from the picnic site. The government doesn't keep tabs on everyone's movements. Why would they?"

"Then how come you picked us up?"

"You're not chipped and clearly not from around here."

"Is it so obvious we're offworlders?" Carina repeated.

Matt's open, honest features creased into a confused expression. "I-I'm not sure."

Jackson's guard leaned close and whispered in his ear. Matt nodded and said firmly, "No more questions."

They arrived at the detention center. After climbing the steps into the building, they passed through two sets of double doors, each requiring a security check from two of the local police officers. Two guards stood on the inside of the inner doors. They scanned the right hands of all the officers before allowing them and the prisoners to pass.

The Bridgeford Police led them downstairs to a lower section, where a woman in uniform sat at a desk. "Murder suspect first."

His guard brought him forward and removed his handcuffs and hobble, she told Jackson to empty his pockets and place everything on the table.

Carina threw Parthenia and Darius a look.

Their backpacks with their supplies remained at the first police station and Jackson said he wasn't carrying anything. His guard confirmed this.

"Search him again," said the woman.

The guard patted him down thoroughly. "He's clean."

Except for the gun in his forearm.

"All right. Put him in cell five." As the guard led him away the woman looked at Carina. "Her next."

Matt brought her over and took off her handcuffs.

"All personal items on the table."

Uh oh. "Can I keep my water? I'm thirsty."

The woman glared at her. "All personal items on the table."

Carina hesitated, taking stock. She could possibly Cast in time to Transport everyone out of here, all the way back to the shuttle. Or she could create a diversion that would allow Parthenia or Darius to do it. But that would give the game away. No doubt their images had been recorded. Casting in front of all these people would give them a rep that would follow them all over the planet.

"If you refuse to comply," the woman said, "this officer will remove the items for you."

With a heavy heart, Carina unfastened the belt that held her elixir canister, folded it, and put it down. Then she pulled from her pockets the sundry bits and pieces she carried to help her Locate her siblings and also placed them on the table.

"That's it?"

She nodded.

The woman scooped everything into a bag then got up and walked around the table. After giving Carina a cursory search, she said to Matt, "Cell nine."

He led her away, taking her to the last cell in the row.

"Are they splitting us up?" she asked.

"They don't mess around in Bridgeford."

Shit.

She and her companions wouldn't even be able to communicate. Being captured on their first day on Earth was bad enough. Now things were getting worse. "We'll see you again, though, right?" The friendly officer might be their only chance of escape.

He grimaced. "I'm sure I'll be around."

The cell door opened. The interior was tiny, just a bunk and a small cupboard. How long would she have to spend here awaiting her fate? Matt's comment about the authorities being on the lookout for offworlders had deeply unsettled her, though she couldn't put her finger on the reason.

"In you go," said Matt, lightly touching her back.

She resisted and glanced up the corridor to where Pamuk's handcuffs were being removed prior to her being processed by the woman at the desk.

"Where's Jackson?" she asked.

"The murderer? Cell five. But you won't be able to talk to him. You have to go inside now." His voice had a slightly pleading tone to it, as if he was reluctant to force her.

"But where exactly is he? I just want to know."

Matt pointed at the blank door diagonally opposite. She spotted the tiny 5 above it.

Memories of Sot Loza were flooding back. Her confinement on that planet hadn't been as bad as it had been for others from the *Bathsheba* but it had been bad enough. Before that the Dark Mage on Magog had tried to trap the mages in his palace. Earlier, the Regians had captured them to turn them into living meals for their offspring. And, in the very beginning of this crazy adventure she'd been living ever since rescuing Darius, the Dirksens and the Sherrerrs had wanted to enslave her and her siblings. There was always someone trying to deprive her and the people she loved of their freedom.

No more.

Matt said, more firmly, "Into the cell, n—"

She slammed her elbow into his stomach. Air exploded from his mouth and he doubled over. She sped down the corridor, hoping he wouldn't be able to shout for a few seconds. Racing into the admissions room, she dove for the bag of her belongings behind the desk, yelling to Darius and Parthenia, "You know what to do!"

She caught a glimpse of Pamuk throwing herself on one of the officers and Bryce attacking the other. Jackson's guard seemed to have left. She got hold of the bag, but the Bridgeford officer snatched it at the same time. They wrestled, the woman yelling at her to let go. Carina managed to open it. She shoved a hand in. Her fingers closed on the smooth, hard elixir canister. She pulled it out, relinquishing the bag. The woman flew backward and landed on her backside. Instantly, she leapt up and ran at Carina, who performed a high kick, connecting with her jaw. The woman's eyes rolled up and she keeled over.

Despite being handcuffed, Darius and Parthenia had managed to drink elixir and were Casting.

"Get away from those people you're fighting!" Carina yelled at Bryce and Parthenia. She unscrewed the lid of the canister and took a swig.

"Hands up!" Matt must have got his breath back and followed her.

She was writing the Character in her mind. Unsure of who Parthenia and Darius were Transporting, she included Bryce and Pamuk. You couldn't over-Transport someone, so it didn't matter.

"Everyone, put your hands up," Matt repeated, "or I'll shoot."

The Character was written. She sent it out.

The last thing she recalled before the Cast took effect was someone grabbing her arm.

8

"**N**ot again!"

Carina opened her eyes. She was back in the forest, next to the clearing where they'd concealed the shuttle. The Cast had worked and she'd escaped imprisonment.

"First Cheepy, and now him," Pamuk complained. "Can't you be a bit more careful?"

She turned around and came face to face with Matt, who had the look of someone suffering a large and unwelcome surprise. *Damn.* Her Transport had carried him along with her. "Sorry about this."

"What the...?" Pale and sweaty, he turned a circle, gaping. "Where am I?"

She checked everyone else had made it before reassuring him. "Don't worry, I didn't bring you far. You can probably walk home from here."

"No, he can't," said Bryce. "Parthenia, could you Unlock me?" He was still wearing handcuffs.

Parthenia replied, "In a minute. I have to do my own."

"I'll do all of us," said Darius.

"Why not?" Carina asked Bryce. "We're back in the—"

"Think."

Matt knew exactly what they'd done, or if not exactly, he knew they'd done *something* to move themselves and him kilometers across the landscape. The other officers back at Bridgeford Detention Center had only seen them disappear. That was bad, though a better alternative than being locked up. But Officer Matt knew more—too much, in fact. "Oh, yeah."

He seemed to be coming to the same understanding, for he was beginning to slowly edge away from the group.

"You should hang around here for a while," Carina said.

Three sets of handcuffs opened and fell to the ground.

He seemed to suddenly recall he had a gun. He lifted it and pointed it at her, then pointed it at each of them in turn, all the while backing up toward the trees.

"Stay here with us," Carina said. "I promise no one's going to h—"

He ran.

Pamuk raced after him only a few steps behind, her boots thumping into the soft leaf litter, and Bryce followed. All three disappeared under the overhanging branches. Loud rustling and the sound of twigs breaking came from under the canopy, and flashes lit up the shadows as Matt fired.

"He won't get away," Parthenia remarked.

"No," Carina agreed.

A corner of the camouflage sheeting over the shuttle lifted and Hsiao emerged. "I thought I heard talking. I wasn't expecting you back so soon. How did it go?"

"Terribly," Parthenia replied.

Darius said, "It only took us a couple of hours to reveal our abilities."

"I think that must be a record," said Hsiao. "Where are the others?"

"Long story," Carina said. "Pamuk and Bryce will be back soon with a visitor. Meanwhile, I have to retrieve Jackson." She swigged elixir.

"Where from?"

"Jail." She closed her eyes.

"Not his first time, I bet."

"Probably."

"Good luck," said Parthenia.

Darius added, "Be careful."

She was within the confined space of Jackson's cell. The merc lay on his bunk, hands behind his head. "What took you so long?"

"I've only been gone five minutes! Stars."

"Where did you go?"

"Back to the..." Her lips snapped shut and she cast a glance around the cell. "Get ready."

Jackson swung his legs over the edge of the bunk and got to his feet.

The cell door opened. The woman who had checked Jackson and her into detention, plus another Bridgeford police officer stood in the entrance.

Damn.

As she'd suspected, the cell was being monitored. She lifted her canister to her lips. "Cover me," she told Jackson from the corner of her mouth.

He pushed up his shirt sleeve.

The female officer gasped, "What are you doing? Put that down! How do you do that? Shoot! Shoot th—"

Carina was in the forest again, her merc friend by her side.

"Hey, Jackson," said Darius.

"Hey, kid." He rolled his shoulders and surveyed his surroundings. "What happened to Pamuk and Bryce? Didn't they make it back?"

"They're fine," Carina replied. "They're around here somewhere."

The undergrowth parted, and Pamuk and Bryce appeared from amongst the foliage, Matt suspended between them. In the scuffle to apprehend him, he'd sustained a cut lip and the skin around one of his eyes was swelling and turning purple. Carina winced. The man hadn't done anything to hurt anyone. He'd just been in the wrong place at the wrong time, or rather, grabbing the wrong person at the wrong time.

"Couldn't you two be more gentle?" she chided.

"Did you want us to capture him or not?" Bryce retorted.

Jackson squinted at the police officer. "Why did you bring *him* along?"

"I didn't do it on purpose. It was an accident."

"You mean like Cheepy?" Jackson shared a look with Pamuk.

"Yes," Carina replied between her teeth. "Like Cheepy."

"Cuff him, Jackson," said Pamuk. She held Matt's gun in her other hand. As she passed the man over, she tucked it into the back of her pants. "What now?"

"Well," said Parthenia, "as our first foray into Earth society was pretty much a disaster, maybe we should return to the *Bathsheba* and rethink our strategy."

Carina sighed. "First of all, let's not discuss our business in front of the prisoner."

"I didn't hear anything," said Matt. "Nothing at all. And I promise, if you let me go, I won't remember anything about any of this."

"So how are you going to explain disappearing along with the rest of us? When you're asked how you managed to arrive in this forest from nowhere, what are you going to say?"

"I-I'll tell them I don't remember. I could say I hit my head." He gestured at his swollen eye.

"And your lip happened to walk into a fist too? No one's going to believe you. I'm sorry, but you're sticking with us, at least until we figure out what to do with you."

He hung his head.

"Don't worry," said Darius. "You won't come to any harm. We're nice people."

"Pamuk isn't," Jackson said.

She shoved his shoulder.

He continued, "And neither are Rees or Van Hasty, come to think of it. And Carter and Blake are absolute ass—"

"That's enough of a rundown on the Black Dogs," Carina interrupted. "Jackson, you stay with the prisoner. Everyone else, over here." After they'd walked some distance away, she went on, "I'm inclined to agree with Parthenia. We need to leave for a while and debrief before thinking up a new way forward. Clearly, just walking into town isn't going to work. We stick out too much."

"And we don't have any idea what we're doing," said Darius.

"There is that too."

"But we can't take the prisoner with us," said Pamuk. "He's seen what you guys do. He's already a liability, and if we take him back to the ship he'll see everything. We'll never be able to let him go. It might be better and kinder to get rid of him now. It's either that or keep him in the brig forever."

Carina sucked in a breath. "I'm fairly confident Officer Matt won't think it's better and kinder to kill him now."

"We can't kill him!" Darius exclaimed. "That would be terrible."

"It's only a suggestion," said Pamuk.

Parthenia said, "We've come a long way over many years and we aren't leaving anytime soon. Who knows what the future holds? It's still early days. We can't leave the prisoner behind so we have to take him with us. After that, we'll have to see how things pan out. But I agree, we can't kill him. There's been enough death on our journey. Let's not sully our endeavor with more of it."

"You're right," said Carina, admiration for her sister swelling in her chest. "You're absolutely right. Okay, the prisoner comes with us."

"If his mind was blown by our Casting," Darius said, "I wonder what he'll make of the *Bathsheba*?"

9

Carina wasn't sure exactly what Officer Matt made of the colony ship as he stepped down from the shuttle, but it wasn't good. She was behind him. All she could see was his back, but it was clear from the way his chest expanded and contracted rapidly he was going through something.

She called out to Bryce, who was walking in front, "Check the prisoner."

He turned just in time to catch Matt as he collapsed. Bryce supported him, holding him under the arms as his head lolled against his shoulder, and then gently eased him down to the deck. Matt was out cold. She guessed traveling to a starship must have been too much of a shock.

The mission members crowded around the prone figure.

"I'll Heal him," said Darius.

"No, get a medic, just in case it's serious. He might have something wrong with him. If he has we need to know what it is."

"It's not my fault," said Pamuk defensively. "I didn't hit him that hard."

Jackson tutted. "Always the guilty conscience."

"I'll comm sick bay," said Hsiao.

By the time the medics arrived Matt was already coming around.

After a quick assessment they decided he'd probably only fainted but they would take him in for 24 hours for observation. Pamuk and Jackson went with them to arrange security.

Ferne and Oriana appeared.

"We heard you were back," Ferne said. "How did it go?"

Oriana added, "We thought you would be gone for days. I take it there was a huge disaster due to the fact we weren't with you."

"There was somewhat of a disaster," Parthenia replied, "but it would have been the same whether you were with us or not."

"Still," Ferne said, "it's our turn next, right, Carina?"

"Nothing's been decided yet. We've only just got off the shuttle, for star's sake. We need to think things through." Though it had been years since his death, she missed Cadwallader more than ever. He would have had a plan B, or at the very least they could have bounced ideas off each other. She also missed Jace and his gentle, steady good sense and kindness.

Oriana whined, "Are you going to tell us what happened or not? You can't leave us hanging."

"I'm exhausted," Parthenia said. "If you want my side of the story you'll have to wait for it. I'm going to lie down for a while."

"I'll tell you," said Darius, "but first I want something to eat."

"You can talk and eat," Ferne said. "Come on."

Carina watched the four siblings walk out of the bay. Bryce wrapped an arm around her and she sighed as she rested her head on his shoulder. "Parthenia's right. That was a huge disaster. What made me think we could just appear on Earth and everything would be fine? That they would accept mages, leave us alone, and we could all live happily ever after?"

"I don't think you ever thought that, did you? We all knew it wouldn't be plain sailing. What we didn't know was what the problems might be."

"I guess you're right. Let's go and eat, preferably somewhere far away from Ferne and Oriana and their interrogation."

They took an elevator to Deck Seven, printed some simple food in a small galley, and went into the Twilight Dome. Luckily, it was empty, possibly because all that could be seen through the transparent overhead was the dusty, rocky, gray, barren surface of Earth's moon. Scan data showed there had once been research stations beneath the surface but all had been abandoned. No humans lived there now who could spot the vast starship in geostationary orbit on its far side.

They sat and began to eat. Carina picked at her noodles and vegetables.

After a few moments Bryce said, "Spit it out."

"Huh?" She paused, her fork poised halfway to her mouth.

"Whatever it is that's bothering you."

She put the fork down. "Isn't it obvious? How are we ever going to make a success of this? The people on Earth are a bunch of weirdos. They grow plants in every available crevice, their police aren't usually armed, and they get around in underground tunnels. I noticed something else, too. There were no fields for crops or for farm animals. How the heck do they eat?"

"We only saw a small area. Maybe there weren't any farms around there. And we only saw a couple of towns in one country. Earth won't be the same all over. No planet is like that. You should know. You've seen enough of them."

"Do you think we should try another country?"

"It wouldn't hurt."

"But the news of what we did in that detention center will be all around the globe by now. They must have vids of us. There were cameras everywhere. Jackson even had one in his cell. So our faces will be known as well as our ability to disappear and reappear at will. Wherever we set foot, we'll be noticed, and then someone will be along to arrest us."

"Maybe we could go somewhere very remote, where there isn't much technology."

"Hmm..." The place where she'd grown up had been similar to what Bryce had described. It had been very poor. No one could afford expensive tech, and few people could afford any tech at all. Nai Nai hadn't had anything to connect her with the outside world. She'd relied on the customers for news about what was going on in the outer world, though Carina suspected her grandmother might have also Sent with other mages. She wouldn't have told Carina about it while she was too young to keep a secret. In fact, that might have been how she knew Ba had died, not because she had a 'feeling'.

"Your food's getting cold," said Bryce.

"I'm not hungry." She put the plate down. "Maybe you're right. Maybe we could go somewhere far from civilization, but what would be the point? The reason we're here is to find a place where mages can live in the open, where we're accepted for who we are, and no one tries to exploit us. If we have to hide away out in the wilds, I'm back to square one. That's how I grew up. It was a better experience than my siblings', at least until Nai Nai died, but it wasn't much of a life. I don't want to live in fear anymore. Is that too much to ask?"

"No, it isn't. But I think you're being too pessimistic. So our first try didn't work out. So what? We can try again. We have a whole planet with billions of people, and we've only just arrived. If you thought everything would be easy, you were expecting a lot. It might take years for humans on Earth to understand your family and learn how to deal with them fairly."

"Ugh, it's already taken us years to get here."

Yet he was right. She *was* being impatient.

"Have you thought about other mages?" he asked.

"Others? On Earth?"

"The documents you found on Ostillon confirmed the old stories that mages came from Earth. Even if they all left the mutation might have reappeared. There might be mages down there, only they don't know what they are."

"They didn't all leave. The documents say some chose to remain but go into hiding." With Nahla's help, over the long years of the voyage, she had translated everything in the ancient papers. Naturally, there was no way to check whether the translation was accurate, but their version made sense.

"There you go," said Bryce. "If the ones who stayed behind passed down their lore the same as the colonizers, there are mages on Earth now who can help you."

"That's a big if. It would have been safer to give up practicing their abilities."

"The mages who left didn't."

"But they had new worlds all to themselves for decades, perhaps centuries, before the ordinary humans caught up to them. They..."

He was giving her a steady stare.

"All right," she conceded. "I guess I am being too negative. Maybe it's because I hate to think of those poor people living there for millennia, frightened of their powers being revealed and suffering the same hatred and persecution as their ancestors. And it would mean that my quest is hopeless, that Earth isn't a safe haven and never will be."

"We've barely arrived, Carina. Stop over-thinking things. We can try again somewhere else. Only we'd better take Ferne and Oriana this time or we'll never hear the end of it."

He continued to eat and she watched him, thankful for his presence in her life. Then something about him distracted her.

After a few moments he noticed. "What's wrong? What are you looking at?" He lifted a hand to the spot above his left ear that was her focus.

"Oh, nothing. Have you finished?" She offered to take his plate.

"Have I got a cut there?" He pressed his fingers against his scalp. "I can't feel anything."

"I forgot to ask you, how did you take down Matt?"

"Pamuk threw a stone to make the undergrowth rustle, and when he fired at it I tackled him from behind. Then Pamuk took over. You know what she's like. But you're changing the subject. What's so interesting about my hair?"

"You...er...you're going gray. Did you know?"

"No, I didn't." A brief look of concern flitted over his features, but then he shrugged. "It's only to be expected, I suppose, after living with you all these years."

She chuckled and playfully punched his arm. "I'm to blame, huh?" Then she grew somber and she continued in a softer tone, "Do you have any regrets? Answer honestly."

He'd left his family behind to be with her, abandoning them with a note to say he was safe but he had something he had to do. That would have been the last his parents and siblings had heard from him, and with the time dilation effects all of them would be long dead.

"No, I made my choice, and you can't live with a choice like that while holding onto regrets. I would have driven myself crazy. And it was the right choice."

"Thanks. I needed to hear that."

"No problem. It's the truth. Hey, we're forgetting something. We don't need to rely on all those quadrillions of bits of data about Earth anymore. We have our own shipboard source of intel now."

"Of course. Officer Matt."

10

Matt was looking better when Carina went to see him a few hours later. He was sitting up in bed, and Ava was fussing over him, adjusting his pillow and pouring water into a cup. The Marchonish woman hadn't spent much time out of Deep Sleep on the long voyage. She'd said she didn't want her little girl to spend most of her childhood living on a starship. But the time she had spent awake she'd asked to be trained as a medic, to give her a source of income when they reached Earth. On Marchon, women had been expected to stay at home and not undertake paid employment, which would bring great shame on their families.

Carina had a soft spot for Ava, who had lived with her siblings on Sot Loza and, to an extent, been a mother figure while Carina could not. Now, her daughter was four years old and Ava had her hands full with working and looking after her. Consequently—and partly also due to the mages spending more time out of stasis—the two families had drifted apart, though Carina still felt warmly toward her, though she remained embarrassed that she'd named her daughter Carina.

"How's our patient?" she asked.

"He's doing very well. All his vitals are normal. It's most likely he suffered a bout of low blood pressure as he disembarked the shuttle. It isn't uncommon in people not used to space travel."

The color had come back to Matt's cheeks and he definitely looked perkier. One of his wrists was handcuffed to the bed frame.

Carina asked, "Is he well enough for a chat?"

"Absolutely. I wouldn't have a problem him being discharged today, but Dr Asher is being cautious as usual. She's given him one of your translators."

Matt's attention was focused on Ava until she'd left the room. When he turned to Carina and Bryce, caution overshadowed his features. "What do you want?"

Carina perched on the side of his bed. "We aren't any happier about this situation than you. I didn't intend to take you with me when I Transported to the forest. It was an accident. But now you're here we're all going to have to make the best of it."

"And what does 'making the best of it' mean exactly?"

"We're not sure yet. As my brother was telling you, we aren't bad people. No one here will hurt you, or at least not unless you force them. You should know most of the people on this ship are trained mercenaries and they haven't had a fight in a very long time."

"You're keeping me here against my will. If that isn't hurting me I don't know what is."

"Believe me, you don't want to find out. Like I said, we haven't come to a decision about what to do with you, but in the meantime perhaps you can help us."

"Why would I do that?"

"Call it doing us a favor."

"I don't owe you anything."

"No, but..." She appealed to Bryce with her eyes.

He sat on the other side of the bed. "Look, friend, you're at a big disadvantage. Carina is trying to be nice because she feels guilty about dragging you into this—"

"I wouldn't call threatening me with mercenaries being nice."

"...but the facts are you're all alone with no way of even contacting anyone, let alone leaving. All anyone knows is that you mysteriously disappeared along with a bunch of prisoners. For all they know, you're in on it with us. Otherwise, why would you disappear too? If you never go back, no one will ever be any the wiser about what happened to you. So it's in your interest to do whatever we say, isn't it? That way, we might be inclined to feel kindly toward you."

Matt shifted uncomfortably, his gaze traveling between them. "What do you want me to help you with?"

"We need to know about Earth," Carina said.

"Earth?" He laughed. "Odd question. It's a big place. Could you whittle that down a bit?" As she tried to decide what would be most useful to know, he went on, "Maybe if you told me who you are and what you're trying to do it would help."

"Ugh, where to start?" She wasn't sure it was safe to tell him *anything*.

"How did you move me from Bridgeford to the forest? I thought you must have drugged me somehow, but you said it happened like I experienced it, disappearing in one place and a second later appearing in another. I've seen it plenty of times on shows, but that's just a trick. You're saying it really happened?"

She didn't answer. Mage powers were the last thing she wanted him to know about.

"Can all aliens do that?" he asked hesitantly.

"Aliens? We're not aliens. We're human, like you."

"But we're on a starship, right? A very big one, from what I can tell. That smaller ship we were on brought us here. Only aliens travel on starships."

"That's not true," said Bryce. "Humans invented space travel millennia ago. We travel on starships all the time."

His eyes lit up. "I get it now! You're members of that cult. What's it called? The Exodus Testifiers. You did drug me. All of this is made up."

"We're...what?"

"Exodus Testifiers. Don't try to deny it. I'll give you credit, though. You had me fooled for a while there."

Bryce said, "What the hell are you talking about?"

"If you let me go now, I'll say you treated me well. You'll get off with a light sentence, maybe just a few months in a psychiatric hospital."

"Matt," Carina said, "what's an Exodus Testifier?"

He laughed again. "Nice. Keep it up. This is hilarious. Where did you get the money for all this? All those props and special effects must have cost a fortune. And are the people members of the cult too, or did you pay actors?"

"We haven't paid anyone anything. This is all real."

"No, it isn't," he said patiently. "I understand you enjoy pretending, but it's time for the games to stop. Kidnapping a police officer is a serious crime, and you can add assault to that charge." He prodded his swollen eye. "You need to release me and you need to do it now, before you get into even more trouble."

He was so earnest, for a brief moment Carina had the weirdest sense that perhaps he was right. Could she be living in an illusion? Could her life up until now be the imaginings of a sick mind? Then she snapped back to reality. "Everything that's happened to you is exactly as it seemed. You were Transported to the forest. You traveled on a space shuttle, and you are aboard a starship. Her name is the *Bathsheba* and she used to be a colony ship. We acquired her in deep space two galactic sectors from here, and we've traveled for decades in stasis to come to Earth."

Matt shook his head in wonder. "It's marvelous how deeply you believe that bullshit, despite all the evidence to the contrary. Tell me, where are you from? And what did you used to do, before you got sucked in I mean?"

Carina locked gazes with Bryce. How could they convince Officer Matt of the truth?

"Maybe we should call Clarkson," Bryce said.

"Yeah, good idea."

The doctor could assess Matt's mental state. He could be experiencing a psychotic break. The shock of all that had happened to him might have placed too much stress on his mind, and this was his way of explaining everything.

"Dr Clarkson will check you over again," she said. "She won't be long."

"No more checks. You must let me go. Now." He rattled his handcuff on the metal bed frame. "People will be looking for me and it won't be long before they trace my chip. You don't stand a chance. Save yourselves and give yourselves up."

Carina rose to her feet. There was no point arguing with him. He was completely convinced he was right.

As she and Bryce walked to the door, Matt shouted after them, "You won't get away with this! Things are going to go very badly for you if you don't release me immediately!"

When they were outside, Bryce went into Clarkson's office while Carina comm'd Nahla.

"Hi, Carina," she replied. "I heard you were back. How did it go?"

"Not great, but I have another problem I'd like your help with. You've been looking at the information we have on Earth, right? Did you notice anything about Exodus Testifiers?"

"What a strange name. No, I don't think so. I'm sure I would remember if I did."

"Could you look it up? Find out everything you can about them."

"Happy to, but why? Is it something to do with mages?"

"No, nothing like that. I accidentally kidnapped a police officer, and he thinks that's what we are. Exodus Testifiers. And unless we can convince him otherwise, I don't think he's going to tell us anything useful about Earth."

"Hold on. Rewind. You accidentally kidnapped a police officer?"

"Don't start. Pamuk gave me enough grief already, all the way back on the shuttle."

11

Though the translations of the mage documents were all on the ship's database and readily accessible via any interface, Carina sometimes liked to handle the ancient papers themselves. There was a sensation of connectedness and deep nostalgia to be had from touching the sheets created by her ancestors thousands of years ago. And she had worked so hard and so much had been sacrificed to attain them. Some people had sacrificed their lives. The documents were precious—priceless, in fact. What value could be placed on something so unique?

She had taken them from the safe and brought them to the cabin she shared with Bryce. In the early days of the journey, a techie had encased the brittle, aged papers in a transparent substance to preserve them, and now they slid easily between her fingers. One by one, she placed them on the bed, spreading them out. The same handwriting had been used on all of them, but the author hadn't signed their name. Similarly, no signature gave away the identity of the artist who had created the sketches of the mages' mountain home, their first attempt at a sanctuary for their kind. Perhaps the writer and artist had been the same person. Had he or she ever imagined that their creations would still exist thousands of years later and be the remaining source of written lore of mages?

The door chimed.

Nahla had come to see her. Carina invited her sister in.

"You got those old papers out again?" Nahla asked, eyeing the unconventional bedspread. "Didn't we squeeze every last drop of knowledge out of them?"

"Yeah, I reckon we did, but I still like to look at them. Can I get you a drink?"

Nahla shook her head. "Don't let me stop you though." She sat at the table. "I like coming here. Ferne and Oriana did a wonderful job with your room."

The twins had excelled as interior decorators during the voyage, expanding on their first vocation as fashion designers. They had printed wall hangings and paintings and created matching textiles for the cabin. Carina had allowed them free rein as an indulgence, which had resulted in a daring mix of colors and patterns, but the effect had grown on her over time.

"You should let them do yours." Carina sat opposite her sister.

Nahla shuddered. "Too risky. It worked with you, but who knows what they might come up with for me? And then I would have to pretend I liked it or they would be offended. Besides, there's no point now. We won't be living here much longer."

"I'm not too sure about that. From what happened on our first try, I think it's going to be hard to do what we want."

"Hmm. I bumped into Parthenia on my way over. She told me a little of what happened. At least no one was hurt."

"That's about the best that can be said. It's nice to see you, but I take it this is more than a social visit." Nahla's preference for research over company was well-known. "Are you here to tell me what you found out about the Exodus Testifiers?"

"You know me too well." She opened the table's interface and navigated to a personal file. After opening it, she turned the display to face Carina. "That was quite the rabbit hole you sent me down. Fascinating stuff. And it throws a whole new light on human civilization on Earth. Read the top entry."

EXODUS TESTIFIERS – Conspiracy theorists or mentally ill?

John Markham (name changed for anonymity) is an unprepossessing man. Pass him in the street and you wouldn't look twice. Grey-haired, mid-fifties and well into middle-aged spread, he's even wearing the trademark cardigan and slacks typical of his generation when he allows me into his home. I ask him if he's married, but Markham is single—perhaps unsurprisingly. It would take a special kind of person to tolerate living with someone so deep into their obsession.

Most of us have a hobby or pastime. Many of us have several. We all need something fun and interesting to do for leisure, whether it be sports, outdoor pursuits, crafts, or more esoteric activities. But few take things to the level John has, and he isn't alone. It's estimated there are more than ten thousand Exodus Testifiers spread across the globe and, what's more, their numbers are growing.

I first came across John's writings on an ancient history forum. That's one of my interests. I'd heard of Exodus Testifiers but I'd never encountered one in the flesh, so to speak. Knowing it wouldn't be long before his words were gone, I copied everything he wrote. Inevitably, the mods banned him about an hour later, but by then I had a treasure trove of his thoughts, beliefs, and, some might say, ravings. I read them avidly, and my eyes were opened to this bizarre cult.

I had to know more. Perhaps I was developing an obsession of my own?

John must have known his opportunity to voice his views to the general public would be brief because he'd given his contact details in one of his posts. No sooner had I found him than a meeting was set up. He seemed eager to introduce a new potential disciple to the fellowship.

His home is testimony to his beliefs. Images of starships adorn every centimeter of the living room wall. Models of the vessels sit on every available surface. He invites me to take a seat, moving aside a pile of odd packages. When I ask what they are, his answer surprises me, even though I thought I knew what I was getting into.

"Rations," he says with a grin. He picks one up. "Freeze-dried curry. Add water and heat it up—after steaming your rice, of course—and, bingo, a healthy meal." He picks up another package. "Ice-cream." He pulled a face. "That one isn't so nice. But if you were in a survival situation it would be very welcome, I'm sure."

"Survival situation?" I ask. "Is that what this is about?"

"That's only a small part of it. Survival just happens to be my particular interest."

"I see. I'm new to this. Would you be able to sum up the core Exodus Testifiers' beliefs in a sentence or two?" I reach into my pocket for my interface. "Do you mind if I record our meeting—for me to listen to later in case I forget anything?"

His expression turns sharp and suspicious. "You aren't a journalist, are you?"

"No, no. Just an interested citizen."

"Only the media has a tendency to make fun of us. Testifying is a serious pursuit. We have plenty of evidence to back up our claims, but academics are too frightened of upsetting the status quo to pay any attention to it. The minute anyone knows you're a Testifier, everything you say is ignored and dismissed."

"I won't make a recording if you don't want me to." I slip the interface back into my pocket.

He relaxes. "One or two sentences? That's hard, but if I had to summarize, I'd say we basically believe that, for a period of two or three thousand years, humans regularly left Earth in order to colonize other worlds."

"Let's be clear. You aren't talking about Mars, Venus, or other planets in the Solar System. You mean planets light years away."

"Exactly."

I decide to humor him. I get the impression that the slightest questioning of his beliefs will make him shut up tighter than a clam. I gesture at the many pictures and models of space-going vessels surrounding us. "In ships like these?"

Carina's jaw dropped. She lifted her gaze to Nahla, who was watching her with amusement. "What did I just read?"

Nahla chuckled. "There's more, if you're interested. Lots more."

"He...doesn't think people ever left Earth?"

"Not just the writer. Most of the population. Exodus Testifiers are the exceptions."

"But how is that possible? It doesn't make any sense. Even if the people on Earth gave up on space exploration, they can't have forgotten about it. There has to be plenty of evidence to show what happened in the past."

"Apparently not. And, thinking about it from a data storage perspective, it isn't so strange. Computer systems change over time. What was accessible a few centuries ago could be completely corrupted or irretrievable now. Data doesn't persist in the same way as those mage documents on your bed. And reporting styles change too. Present-day archaeologists might misinterpret an ancient media report about a colony ship's departure as fiction rather than fact."

"But what about shipyards? They're huge. There has to be something left of them."

"Most starships are built in space, remember. They would have fallen to Earth, probably crashing into an ocean. There might be something left of component manufacturing plants, but an excavation wouldn't necessarily reveal the exact purpose of the discovered artifacts. That would be open to interpretation, and people tend to explain evidence in the context of their culture and perspective."

The enormity of the misunderstanding was hard to swallow, but one thing was clear: Officer Matt genuinely thought they were crazy cultists, living out a fantasy. She didn't know how to persuade him to accept that he and most of the rest of humanity was wrong. Whatever they showed him, he would believe it was an illusion. If they took him on a tour of the ship, he would think it was an impressive set. If they showed him the view from the Twilight Dome, he would say it was a vid.

"So," said Carina, "if we were to go to Earth and announce that we were space travelers from another galactic sector, the descendants of colonizers who left millennia ago, no one would believe us?"

"Not only that, there's a good chance you would be locked up—for your own good. As the article implies, Exodus Testifiers are often believed to be mentally unwell."

"But what if we showed them the *Bathsheba*? No one could deny we were telling the truth then."

"Right, but if you did that, how long do you think you could hold onto her? The arrival of an actual starship from outer space would blow apart the current understanding of humankind's history. My impression so far of Earth societies is that they're generally friendly, non-violent, and free. But that doesn't mean someone won't decide the shockwave of the revelation would be dangerously destabilizing, and seek to remove the evidence from scrutiny. And let's not forget about all of the *Bathsheba*'s tech and weaponry. Less well-meaning individuals would be very keen on getting their hands on them."

Carina rubbed her temples. "We could hold them off, but not forever." And announcing their presence in such a loud fashion was the last thing she wanted. "Thanks for doing the research. The results have been illuminating to say the least."

"It wasn't difficult, and it was fun. I'm sorry if I've created more problems for you." Nahla rose to her feet.

"It's better I'm aware of them now than find out the hard way."

"Let me know if there's anything else I can help you with."

As Nahla left, Carina had a brief vision of a small, frightened girl, recently released from her Dark Mage elder brother's control and traumatized from being trapped in a shuttle cabin with Stevenson's body. She'd come a long way. She was now a confident young woman and the smartest person on the ship. She deserved a good, happy, fulfilling life. They all did. But the chances of achieving it were looking increasingly remote.

Carina returned to the mage documents spread over her bed. How to turn what she knew into a successful outcome? How could they integrate into Earth society safely and live openly, without hiding fundamental aspects of themselves?

Her gaze alighted on the drawings depicting the mages' mountain hideaway. It had to be ruins by now, if any of it remained at all. It was doubtful she would learn anything useful there, yet she had a hankering to visit anyway, if only to walk in the places her ancestors had trodden, imbibing their spirit. But no location was given—understandably, considering the dangers they'd faced.

She tilted her head. Surrounding the stone-walled edifice was the mountain landscape. The lines of the ridges stood out clearly against the sky. Buildings, towns, and cities rose and fell, constructed by humans and destroyed by nature. But mountains didn't change for tens of thousands of years, or at least not significantly.

She comm'd Nahla. "There's something else I'd like you to do."

12

Carina pulled the copy of the mage document from her bag, studied it, and then scanned the view. Thick gray cloud cloaked the sky, obscuring the mountain peaks. Snow glinted on the highest peaks.

Oriana peered over her shoulder. "This is it. It has to be. Look, Ferne. What do you think?"

Her twin, without asking, took the sheet from Carina's hands and frowned over it before handing it back. His eyes narrowed as his gaze swept the view. "Maybe. But I wouldn't get your hopes up. After all this time, there won't be anything left."

"That isn't the point," Oriana countered. "That's right, isn't it, Carina?"

She shivered, turned up the collar of her coat, and pulled her hat lower. She was already regretting bringing her brother and sister along, but without a good excuse she hadn't been able to say no. The twins were intense and had only grown more so during the voyage. Just being around them was tiring.

In truth, she didn't know how to answer the question. She had no good reason for being here except that she had to do *something*. Parthenia, in the interests of having a mage aboard the ship, had stayed behind this time. So had Pamuk, Jackson, and Bryce. They were known to Earth authorities—as was she, but this whole thing was her idea. It was her responsibility to make it work.

Though the rest of the Black Dogs and the Marchonish women were gagging to visit Earth, she'd decided to limit the new away team to Darius, herself, the twins, and Hsiao. They needed Darius to Cloak the shuttle but he was staying with it, along with Hsiao. Until they knew more about the local systems it wasn't safe for anyone from the *Bathsheba* to be here. Matt had said they were 'not chipped'. Any one of them could quickly be spotted as an 'alien' and picked up. On the other hand, they were on an entirely different continent, so who knew what might happen?

"Carina," Oriana repeated, "did you hear me?"

"I heard you. You're right. I don't expect to find the hideaway." However, the mountains in the place Nahla had suggested did match the sketches made by a mage thousands of years ago. The habitation the mages built had sat in a high pass, which was indicated on the drawings but obscured from view when looking from below. "I think there's a path over there."

Hsiao had landed the shuttle as close to the site as possible, but in the rocky landscape they still had many kilometers to travel. It was exactly as the mages had intended. They'd deliberately made their home difficult to reach in order to discourage unwanted visitors. Any non-mages who made it there were turned away, and sometimes they died in the wilderness. That had been the start of the enmity toward mages, the beginning of the motivation behind their exodus.

Exodus Testifiers.

Did they believe in mages too? Or did they only know about ordinary humans' galactic colonization attempts? Would it be worth talking to a Testifier?

"We should Transport up there," said Ferne.

They were nearing the narrow gap in the undergrowth Carina had spotted.

"Is that wise?" Oriana asked.

If you didn't know exactly where you were going, Transport was a little risky. One time, Carina had ended up waist-deep in a swamp.

"There's nothing between us and our destination except trees," Ferne replied. "What could possibly go wrong?"

"Don't say that," Oriana warned. "That's inviting trouble."

"We could leapfrog from here to that slope over there. That'll halve the distance we have to travel."

"I don't suppose it'll hurt," said Carina. The less time spent trekking the better, for several reasons. She pointed out a particularly tall pine. "I'll take us all there." She sipped elixir, Cast, and then opened her eyes, instantly tumbling over and landing on her side in thick leaf litter.

Oriana had done the same.

Ferne laughed. "You two are hilarious. Didn't you realize the ground would be at an angle?"

Carina got to her feet, brushing dead pine needles from her clothes. "Next time, you're Transporting us." She helped her sister up.

It was darker among the tall, overshadowing trees, and the air was colder. Her ears had popped as she'd arrived.

"Smart move," Oriana grumbled. "Now we can't see where to go. Which way is the pass?"

"It would have been the same if we'd walked here," Ferne retorted, "only we would be a lot more tired."

With the sun obscured by a blanket of cloud, it was hard to tell directions, but one thing Carina did know, and that was they had to go up. "This way."

She headed up the slope, weaving through the trees. They didn't grow thickly at this altitude, and if her guess was correct, they would soon thin out before disappearing altogether. Her years aboard a starship were taking their toll. She toiled upward, puffing and panting, hearing the gasping breaths of Ferne and Oriana behind her. Soon, she was sweating despite the cold.

"Maybe..." Oriana said "we should...take a...chance...and—"

"Forget it," Carina said. "We could Transport to an edge of a precipice and fall off."

"And perform the fastest Transport ever before we hit the bottom," added Ferne.

As Carina had predicted, the trees soon disappeared. They scrambled over rocks and slipped on shale as they drove themselves steadily upward.

"We could do lots of small jumps," Oriana called out.

Her voice sounded distant.

Carina halted and turned. Her sister stood about thirty meters down the slope, leaning on a boulder.

Ferne yelled, "We would use up all our elixir, silly. Come on, it can't be far now."

"I don't suppose someone could carry me?"

They ignored her in the way only siblings well-used to—and tired of—their brother's or sister's shenanigans could. In a few moments the sound of Oriana's dogged footsteps came from behind as she crunched her way over the stones. Somehow, she managed to convey her annoyance in every step.

When they reached the pass it appeared suddenly. One minute they were working their way up yet another steep rise, one of seemingly countless others, and the next flat ground stretched out before them. The area separated two steep mountainsides and was strewn with loose rock. In the gap a sliver of blue sky peeked from the lowest stretch of the pass. Everywhere else was gray, misty, and chill.

"We've found it," Oriana breathed. "It has to be it."

Carina pulled the document from her backpack. Next to the image showing the view of the mages' hideaway from afar was a close-up version. "No, it's wrong. We've come the wrong way. *Damn*."

"Let me look."

She handed the sheet to Ferne and then sat on the cold ground, exhausted.

They were clearly in the wrong place. The document showed a bigger area and an outer section of the building, where the mages would receive visitors and test their abilities before either welcoming them or sending them away, depending on the results. Though it might be too much to expect that anything would be left of the mages' construction, the mountainside shouldn't have changed very much. This place was markedly narrower. She guessed there was another pass between another pair of mountains in the range, or perhaps Nahla's suggestion was incorrect.

"You silly goose," said Ferne. "This *is* it." He squatted down beside her and pointed at the spot in the picture where the mountain slopes met. "The angles of the slopes are identical to how they are now."

"Maybe, but there's nowhere near the same amount of space. How could the mages have fitted *that* here?" She prodded the curved protuberance with its wide double doors and window slits. The image showed two figures at the door, giving a clue to the building's size. "There's no way there's room."

He straightened up and gazed from one slope to the other. "But it was so long ago..." he mused. He thrust the toe of his boot into the ground, sending up a spray of rock shards and dust.

"Hey," Carina protested, "watch out!"

"This has all fallen from the slopes, weathered away by the elements. Do we know how long ago mages left Earth?"

"Cadwallader estimated it once. He said it was about seven thousand years ago, based on Jace's knowledge of the number of generations who had lived in our sector."

"Cadwallader? So that must have been before we were kidnapped by the Regians, and since then we've been forced even more light years off course. With time dilation, we can add at least another thousand years to the figure. Eight thousand years." His chin tilted up as his attention focused on the surrounding mountains again. "A lot of rock could have fallen in that time, enough to narrow the pass considerably."

Carina got up, brushing rough pebbles from her backside. Could he be right? The angles of the slopes *were* the same.

"You two!" Oriana called, stepping out from behind a rock.

Carina hadn't noticed she'd disappeared.

"While you've been slacking off," Oriana said, "*I've* been working. I've found a cave entrance. Come and take a look. It seems to go back really far."

13

The cleft in the mountainside was barely wide enough to pass through. They all had to take off their backpacks and edge sideways. Once they were inside, however, the gap quickly opened up. Carina found herself standing in a space the size of a small room. The ground was flat and sandy, and the walls... She stepped closer. The walls resembled others she'd seen before, on a planet far distant half a lifetime ago. "This is it," she whispered. "They were here."

The walls were smooth and polished, like the pebbles Nai Nai used to make, and like the walls in the mountain castle on Ostillon where she'd found the mage documents. Whatever Cast had been used to create the surfaces, hollowing out the mountains' interiors, had been lost as far as she knew. Certainly, Nai Nai hadn't taught it to her and neither had Ma taught it to her siblings. But the similarity was unmistakable.

"Yay!" Oriana exclaimed. "We found it!" She hugged her brother and then Carina, but Carina couldn't return the gesture.

All energy had drained from her limbs and she felt numb.

"It's like the place the Dirksens took over, isn't it?" Ferne asked.

She nodded.

"That's right," said Oriana, running her fingertips over a wall. "I remember now."

He and Oriana had been around thirteen years old when they'd gone with Carina to find the documents. They'd fought alongside the Black Dogs, and they'd been present when Sable Dirksen had shot Darius. It was no wonder the place had left an indelible mark on their memories.

"I need to sit down," Carina said. She walked to the edge of the chamber and slumped to the floor. Burying her face in her hands, she wept.

"What's wrong?" Ferne asked. "I would have thought you would be happy."

"Oh, shut up," Oriana admonished. "She is happy. She's just having a moment." She sat beside Carina and put an arm over her shoulders. "Take as long as you like. We have all day to explore, and now we know where it is, we can come back whenever we like."

Carina sniffed and mumbled, "Thanks."

In fact, she wasn't sure she was crying with happiness. She wasn't sure what she felt. Images of Nai Nai and Ma had flooded her mind, along with the faces of all the people who had died during their journey. She wished she could pull herself together and do what she'd come to Earth to do, but the ghosts of the past seemed to always drag at her, holding her back.

"Have you noticed something?" Ferne asked. "It's light. It should be much darker in here. There's hardly any light coming from the way in, but we can see perfectly well. The walls and ceiling must be faintly glowing." As he'd been speaking he'd wandered around the chamber. "There's a way out," he said as he reached a protuberance. "I'm going to see what else is here."

"Wait," said Oriana. "We shouldn't split up."

"Don't worry. If you can't find me, shout, and if I don't hear you, Locate me."

"Ugh, he's so inconsiderate."

"He's just excited," said Carina. "I'm feeling better now. Let's see what he's found."

On the other side of the protuberance was an arched doorway carved into the rock. There was no question now that *someone* had lived here, if not the mages. And if it was the mages, had they left anything behind?

The opening led to a tunnel with similar doorways at regular intervals. Ferne was peering into one. "Nothing here, just empty rooms. I wonder what they used to be for?"

"What's that noise?" Oriana asked.

"What noise?" Ferne wrinkled his brow. "I can't hear a thing."

"Shhh! Listen."

Carina heard it too: a faint soughing like the wind in a forest, rustling the leaves and branches.

"Oh, yes," said Ferne. "It's coming from that way." He strode down the tunnel, leaving Carina and Oriana hurrying to catch up.

"Slow down," Oriana complained. "We're already exhausted from all the climbing."

Typically, Ferne took no notice. If anything, he seemed to speed up. "It's getting louder," he called over his shoulder. "We're on the right track."

The tunnel sloped downward, diving deep into the mountain. In her hurried glimpses of the rooms they passed, Carina saw only empty, bare spaces. Whatever had once been inside had either been taken by the mages or decayed to dust.

Meanwhile, the noise was growing louder and becoming more distinct. It didn't sound like the wind anymore. It sounded like—"

"Whoa!" Ferne had halted at a portal larger than the others, seemingly transfixed by what lay beyond.

A gust of cool, moist air hit Carina, and she knew her guess at what the noise was had been correct. She joined Ferne at the opening. In a high cavern, the sides lit by the same glowing material that illuminated the place, a waterfall cascaded into a deep, dark pool.

"This must have been why they chose it," Oriana said excitedly, clapping her hands. "An endless supply of water to make elixir."

It had occurred to Carina on the way up that the mountain was a dry place, devoid of the brooks and rills she would have expected to see. It seemed clear that the majority of the snow melt and rainfall in the higher regions was funneled inside the mountain, emerging in this cavern.

"Marvelous," said Ferne, stepping over to the pool. "I'm going to try some."

"Are you sure it's safe?" Oriana asked.

He stooped and scooped a handful of water into his mouth. After swallowing, he gasped. "It's freezing. I felt it all the way down to my stomach." He smacked his lips. "Tastes nice, though."

"You're probably going to catch a horrible disease," said Oriana, "or a parasite."

"Why? The mages must have drunk this all the time."

"They would have boiled it to make elixir, and to drink too."

He pulled a face. "Oh well, if I get sick I'll Heal myself."

Carina?

Darius was Sending to her.

Hey, sweetie. What's up?

Did you find the hideaway?

We're pretty sure we did. We're here now, inside the mountain. It took us a while, but—

I think you should leave.

Huh? Why? We only just got here.

I have a bad feeling. I don't know what it is, but it's coming from near where you are.

"Who are you talking to?" Oriana asked.

"It's Darius. He's saying we have to get out right away. He has a bad feeling."

Ferne scoffed, "He's always having a bad feeling about one thing or another. It's probably indigestion."

"It might be something serious," Oriana replied doubtfully.

"We should listen to him," said Carina. The twins might have forgotten Darius as a little boy saving all their lives more than once, but she hadn't. "Get ready to Transport back to the shuttle."

"What could possibly be dangerous in here?" Ferne asked, opening his arms wide. "We've only just arrived. There must be lots more to see."

"I'm not going to argue," Carina said. "If you won't Transport yourself I'll do it for you."

It went against mage code to Cast on others without their permission, but when it came to protecting her siblings she was prepared to make an exception.

"*Fine.*" Ferne snatched his elixir flask from its holder.

"We can always come back later," Oriana placated.

There was movement on the far side of the cavern. Three figures had appeared at the entrance.

"Who's that?!" Oriana had seen them too.

"Hurry up." Carina swallowed elixir, her gaze fixed on the figures. In her peripheral vision she saw her brother and sister Casting.

One of the newcomers raised his hand and pointed. They'd been seen. Nothing of what was said on the other side of the cavern could be heard over the rushing of the waterfall. One of the other men was doing something else.

Closing her eyes, she wrote the Character in her mind and sent it out. At the same time, she retained what she'd just seen.

The figures were all male. They'd been standing in the shadow of an overhang, which obscured them almost to silhouettes. She hadn't been able to tell their ages or even what they were wearing. All she'd been able to see was the man pointing, and the other one... He'd been drinking from a container! Had he been Casting?

Had his Cast activated before their own, Transporting them to another destination?

She opened her eyes.

There was grass beneath her feet. The air was warm and dry. There were voices.

"Carina," Oriana said, "you made it, thank goodness. Who were those people?"

"Where's Ferne?" she asked, turning. "Is he here?"

"Yes, I'm here. No need to tell me off," he added ruefully. "Darius was right and I was wrong."

Darius was here too, and so was Hsiao. Beneath the camouflage sheet, a tiny piece of the shuttle peeked out. Everyone was safe.

"I don't know who those people were," she said, "but one thing's for sure—they weren't there to welcome us with open arms. It's time we went back to the ship."

14

"Y ou said we were from offplanet," Carina leaned closer to Matt, causing him to edge backward. "What did you mean? You don't believe humans have ever left Earth. Why would you say we're offworlders?"

His comment had come back to her as she'd traveled from Earth to the *Bathsheba*.

"I-I was being sarcastic."

"Sarcastic about what? That we were offworlders?"

"Y-yes!"

"Carina," Darius said, "give him some room, then maybe he'll be able to answer you properly."

They were in the brig, where Matt had been taken after his discharge from sick bay.

Carina moved away from his bunk and folded her arms. "Is this better?"

Matt swallowed. "A little."

Darius asked gently, "Can you explain why you made that comment?"

"I didn't really think you were from outer space..." The Earth man shifted in his seat and plucked at the cuff of his shirt "...though what I've seen here has made me question that."

Was he trying to mollify them, thinking that if he played into their Exodus Testifier fantasy they would treat him well?

"I was referring to the General Alert. You must know it." He added hastily, "Though of course if you really are aliens you wouldn't have heard of it."

"Just tell us what it is," said Carina.

"The General Alert is the warning everyone learns at school, to be on the alert for aliens masquerading as regular people. When the sensors in the wood picked up the presence of humans who weren't chipped, we joked about it at the station."

"Not chipped?" Before he could explain, Carina went on, "Oh, I get it. You have ID chips embedded in your hands." She'd recalled the police officers having their hands scanned. "Everyone on Earth has them?"

"Nearly everyone. Every so often someone turns up who had theirs removed. People who want to disappear for whatever reason. Sometimes they can't get a fake one or it doesn't work. It's against the law, so we arrest them. Before we could process you, your friend killed one of my colleagues. Then things got serious."

"We're sorry about that," Carina said. "You see, where we come from violence is normal. Jackson was only trying to protect himself."

Matt didn't answer. He probably thought she was indulging in her delusion.

"I'm interested in the General Alert," said Darius. "How long has it been in place?"

"I don't know. Since before I was born."

"And it involves being aware that aliens might be walking among you disguised as ordinary humans?"

"Basically."

"How would you be able to tell who these aliens were?"

"Well, for one thing they wouldn't be chipped, hence the joking at the station."

"What else?" asked Carina.

"They would be able to do things humans can't."

"Like?" Darius prompted.

"Like start fires spontaneously, open locked doors, disappear from one place and reappear in an—" He gave a small gasp. His wide-eyed gaze traveled from Darius to Carina and back again. He looked down. "No," he said softly, as if speaking to himself. "No, it can't be." He looked up and grinned nervously. "Neat trick."

"Where does the warning come from?" Carina asked.

"I don't know."

"You said you learned it at school. Does that mean it isn't serious? Is it a boogeyman thing?"

"No, it's serious. I guess it must come from the government. I never really thought about it, but I've seen the warning on websites, notices, that kind of thing."

"If we give you access to Earth information channels, could you find an example?"

Hope bloomed in his features.

"You'll only be able to browse."

Hope faded. "Okay, I'll try."

They left the brig and walked in silence. There was no need to state the obvious. The situation was the last Carina had expected. If she'd discovered that mages were known about and feared on Earth she would have been disappointed but not surprised. But a society prepped to hate and fear them? How had it come about and why? And why weren't they given their real name, rather than portrayed as aliens?

She comm'd Nahla.

"You're back? Good trip?"

"No."

"Oh dear. Maybe next t—"

"While you were looking at the Earth data, did you come across something called the General Alert?"

"Doesn't ring a bell. I can do a search."

"What about warnings to watch out for aliens?"

"No...wait. Yes, I did see one. I thought it was a joke."

Great. "Could you check for the General Alert? And anything to do with aliens with special powers."

"On it."

Darius said, "We need to do something with Matt. We can't keep him here forever. He hasn't done anything wrong or tried to hurt us."

"He locked us up!"

"He was only doing his job."

"Well, what do *you* think we should do with him?"

"The next time we go to Earth, we should take him with us and leave him somewhere safe. He'll be able to make his way home."

"But then what? He'll tell everyone about the *Bathsheba* and all the people on it—the 'aliens'. Then everyone will be on the lookout for us wherever we go."

"Will he tell them we're aliens? Or will he say we're a bunch of crazy Exodus Testifiers who pulled a stunt on him? That's what he seems to believe."

"He might believe that, but there's the evidence of us disappearing from the detention center and Jackson disappearing from his cell a few minutes later. Matt might not believe what really happened, but he'll find it hard to explain those disappearances, and his superiors will expect him to explain. You can be sure about that. In fact, things might be even worse for him than we thought. We—I—brought him with us. The police might think he was colluding with us."

"Hmm," Darius mused. "Didn't think of that. I guess he'll have to stay here a while, until we can think of a way of getting him home without creating problems for him."

Van Hasty appeared in the passageway. "I want to talk to you, Lin, face to face."

Darius said, "Uhh, I'll see you later."

He often escaped when an emotionally charged moment was imminent, and from the merc's expression, it seemed this moment was about to be especially so.

"What do you want?" Carina asked cautiously.

"I want to know exactly when the Black Dogs are gonna set foot on the first freaking planet we've arrived at in ten years."

"It's too soon for you all to go down there. You know that."

"Is it? It might be too soon for you guys, but we don't have your agenda. There's no reason we can't have some R&R."

"There are plenty of reasons. For one thing, you don't have

embedded ID chips like everyone else on Earth. The minute you try to go anywhere, get a job or whatever, people are going to start asking you some very hard questions."

"So what? We'll just say we're from offplanet. There's no law against it."

"You don't underst—"

"We're going stir crazy. We've *been* stir crazy for years. Now the waiting's over and we're at our destination. We expect to get off the ship. Soon. If you keep stalling, something bad's gonna happen."

"Like what?" Carina asked, putting her hands on her hips. "Are you threatening to mutiny?"

Van Hasty's eyes narrowed. "No one ever made you captain. You took that on all by yourself. It's hard to mutiny when you don't have anyone to mutiny against."

Carina took a breath and exhaled. Van Hasty, like many of the mercs, could flip into anger on a trigger switch. It was time to de-escalate. "If the Black Dogs go planetside they could jeopardize everything we've worked for. As it is, our presence is a secret. I want to keep it that way for now. I need to figure some things out. As soon as I have, you all get your R&R. Permanently."

It was a long way back to inhabited regions of the galaxy.

"When? How long is it gonna take you to figure things out?"

"I don't know. I can't give you a date."

"You've got a week. No longer. After that, we take things into our own hands." Van Hasty walked away.

"Hey, wait! You can't hand out an ultimatum. You don't even know the situation down there."

"One week, Lin." She was nearing the bend in the passageway.

"I'll tell Hsiao to refuse to fly you down!"

"We've got Bibik, and, anyway, Hsiao isn't as much on your side as you might think." Van Hasty was gone.

Carina's hands fell to her sides.

15

Ferne and Oriana lounged on cushions on the floor, Parthenia and Darius were on Carina and Bryce's bed, and Nahla and Bryce sat at the small table.

Darius shifted sideways to make room. "Do you want to sit here?" he asked Carina.

"No, thanks. I'll stand." She knitted her fingers. "Are you all sure no one knows where you are?"

"Bibik doesn't know," Parthenia said, "but I'm not happy about it."

She'd been in a relationship with Hsiao's co-pilot for over three years. Nahla and Ferne also had serious partners, and Carina felt bad asking them to keep the meeting a secret from them. "I appreciate whatever little white lies you've had to tell, and I promise this won't be forever, but I don't feel like we have a choice. The Dogs are turning against us. If they knew we were holding a mages-only meeting they might take it the wrong way."

"Bryce and I aren't mages," Nahla said brightly.

"You're honorary mages," said Ferne.

Carina said, "You're family. Maybe that's what I meant."

"And Bibik isn't my family?" Parthenia asked archly.

"You know what I mean. Please don't make this any harder. I'm doing my best to find a home for us, a *real* home. But it isn't working out. I need your help."

"We'll do everything we can to help you," said Darius. "Just tell us what you need."

"That's the problem. I don't know what I need. I don't know what to do. Those three men turning up at the hideaway, and Matt's revelation about the General Alert has thrown everything into question."

Ferne eyed her. "You're *positive* you saw one of those men Casting?"

"A hundred percent."

"*I* didn't. Did you, Oriana?"

She shook her head. "Sorry, Carina, but all I saw was some shadowy figures. They could have been anyone and they could have been doing anything. It was too dark to see."

"When you say you saw one of them Casting," said Bryce, "what do you mean? Only, to someone who doesn't know what you're doing, it just looks like you're taking a drink and closing your eyes."

"That's right," Nahla said. "If I hadn't grown up with mages, I might not even make the connection between what you do and the effect of the Cast. How do you know he wasn't simply drinking something?"

"Don't you think it's a weird thing to do?" Carina asked. "You find some strangers in a cavern and the first thing you do is quench your thirst?"

Parthenia shrugged. "It isn't *that* strange."

"All right." Carina gritted her teeth. "What about Darius's bad feeling about them? When has he ever been wrong?"

"Can you tell us any more about that, Darius?" Parthenia asked. "Did you get any indication of what the men intended, or anything else?"

"Very little, sorry. The feeling was faint—due to the distance, I guess."

Carina said, "The fact that he felt anything at all at that distance tells me at least one of those men is extremely malevolent. Perhaps they all are. And they wished us harm."

"How do you know?" Parthenia asked.

"I just do."

"So you're a Spirit Mage now?"

Darius raised his hands placatingly. "Let's not argue. We need to help Carina, and each other, if we're ever going to live on Earth."

"I'm just concerned that we act based on reality and don't allow ourselves to be spooked by meaningless shadows. We have enough problems facing us without inventing more. There are these ID chips the police officer mentioned, and the fact that the population is on the watch for evidence of Casting."

"Exactly," said Carina. "Doesn't that strike you as oddly specific? Who has been priming them and why?"

"It *is* odd," Parthenia conceded, "but for now all it tells me is that we need to be careful. We can't give anyone cause to even suspect our abilities."

"But we've been forced to be careful all our lives," protested Carina. "Earth is supposed to be our chance for something new."

"Perhaps, with time, we can introduce the idea that mages aren't anything to be feared, and that there's a lot we can do to help people, providing we're allowed to live our lives as we please."

"Stars," Carina muttered. Parthenia sounded so naive. Had she forgotten all the trials and difficulties they'd faced as mages in the past? Had she forgotten everything Ma had gone through? "Before that incident in the mountain, I might have agreed with you that was a possible way forward. Now, it sounds futile and dangerous. It's clear that someone's been waiting for mages to turn up, someone who wants ordinary people to view us as enemies. Think about it. Those men arrived soon after us at the hideaway. Somehow, they knew we were there and they came to challenge us. At least one of them is a mage too. If his Cast had worked before ours, who knows what might have happened?"

"His alleged Cast," Ferne commented.

"Whatever. I'll take that seat." She flopped down on the bed between Darius and Parthenia.

"I found out some information about the General Alert," Nahla said.

"Shoot."

"The earliest instance I can trace occurred fifty-one years ago. It started in one country and gradually spread across the globe over fifteen years or so. Now, it's given out to most schoolchildren up to the age of fourteen. Then, the public information notices take over. They appear where most adults would see them fairly regularly. It seems to be an effort at subliminal programming to be on the lookout for activity that defies known physical laws, as mages do."

She added, ruefully, "Transporting out of the detention center as you did is exactly the kind of thing that would attract a great deal of attention, even more than it would somewhere the General Alert didn't exist. Actually, it already has. I thought I would check for repercussions, and they're all over the place. The recording of the incident has gone viral. Your faces must have been seen by everyone on the planet."

"Fantastic," Carina said. "So much for keeping a low profile."

"I'm glad we *didn't* go with you now," said Oriana.

"We would have been famous—for all the wrong reasons," Ferne quipped.

Carina straightened up. "I suppose there are warrants out for our arrest, Nahla?"

"What do *you* think?"

Ferne said, "It was lucky no one saw you or Darius when we went to the mage hideaway."

"*Some* people saw me," said Carina.

The room fell silent. No one appeared to have anything else to offer the discussion.

If they went planetside they would be apprehended, if not on sight then when it became clear they weren't chipped. It was a disaster. Everything was working against them. And it felt personal. It was as if someone had deliberately arranged things to make Earth the last place mages could live safely.

She announced, "Whoever organized the General Alert has to be connected to the people we saw inside the mountain. This is all too much of a coincidence."

"How do you figure *that*?" Oriana asked. "Nahla said the alert started decades ago. We've only just arrived."

"I can't explain it. It just makes sense. Someone is out to get us, and they nearly did. If it weren't for Darius's warning they would have succeeded. There's only one thing to do. I have to go back to the mountain. I want to find out who those men are and get to the bottom of what they have against us."

"That's insane!" Bryce exclaimed. "If you're correct you'll be walking right into their hands. And Darius has told us they're evil. It's a suicide mission."

"What alternative is there? Until I fix this problem Earth is off-limits. Our voyage will be a waste of time, and all those people who died to get us here will have died for nothing. I can't turn around and go back. I would be making those sacrifices meaningless." She swallowed hard and blinked away tears.

Darius put a hand on her arm. "They're gone, Carina. Nothing you do will affect them."

"It affects *me*."

A second silence fell.

"I'll go with you," said Parthenia.

"What?"

"I'm coming with you. As you said, we won't solve this mystery any other way. And if it comes to a mage battle you'll need another mage on your side. I can repel his Casts with Repulse while you defeat him."

"I thought you said we shouldn't be spooked by meaningless shadows."

"And I meant it. How else am I supposed to discover whether I'm right if I'm not there to see with my own eyes?"

Carina got to her feet and crossed the room to her sister, leaning down to hug her. "It'll be like old times. Do you remember when we blew up the Twilight Dome with Mezban's bomb?"

"How could I forget? It was the first time you didn't treat me like I was a silly little girl who needed protecting from herself."

Ouch.

If there was one thing Parthenia could be relied upon for it was speaking her mind.

"Those days are long gone," Carina said. "It'll be dangerous, but I would love it if you'd come."

16

Everything was the same as before. The mountainside was quiet except for the wind passing over the rocky slopes, and there was no sign of the men. Carina paused at the gap that led into the ancient mage hideaway. The atmosphere had taken on a different feeling. Previously, she'd begun to accept this really was the home of her ancestors. She's started to enjoy a sense of awe and wonder from being here. Then the strange men had arrived and forced her to flee. Now, the dimness beyond the cleft seemed ominous and threatening.

"This is it?" Parthenia asked, peering in.

"We thought so. The shape of the slopes matches the sketch, only the pass is smaller. Ferne thinks it's due to erosion. The outer keep is entirely gone, but Oriana found this entrance. What's inside is like the mountain castle on Ostillon where we found the documents."

"That doesn't sound conclusive."

"No, but… It feels right. It feels as though they were here."

"Hmpf." Parthenia didn't say more, letting the skeptical vocalization stand.

"And the walls glow in a way I can't explain."

"That doesn't mean someone else can't explain it, someone who knows about these things. There could be a perfectly rational explanation. And I've never heard of a Glow Cast. Have you? How would it last all these years?"

Ignoring the unanswerable question, Carina said, "We saw the men fairly deep inside, in a large chamber with a waterfall. I don't know how they knew we were there. I'm worried that entering the cave set off an alarm, and that if we go in we'll do the same, only this time they'll arrive faster. There could even be someone waiting for us. It's only been a few days."

"How do you know the men don't simply live in the caves and your arrival spooked them?"

"I don't know for sure, but everything from here to the waterfall was uninhabited. I'm sure of it. There was dust over everything. No one had been there in a very long time. And look around you. There's nothing here. How could anyone survive here unless they were mages?"

"Well, we *want* the men to arrive. We need to find out who they are."

"We do, but we have to be in control of the situation this time. No more surprises." They'd brought sidearms along this time. The holster on Carina's hip felt awkward. It had been a long time since she'd been involved in a firefight, and though everyone on the *Bathsheba* had kept up with their training, she didn't relish the thought of engaging in armed combat.

"Then why don't we Transport in?" asked Parthenia. "If walking into the cave triggers an alarm we can avoid it. You can take us both to the waterfall."

"All right. Let's do that." Carina swigged elixir and sent out the Cast.

As she opened her eyes, the cool, humid air of the cavern hit her and the thunder of falling water filled her ears. She'd Transported them to the place she'd been standing when she'd spotted the men. She checked the opening on the far side of the waterfall, but it was empty. So far, so good.

Parthenia was already stepping away from her, heading for the pool. "It's quite something, isn't it?" She'd raised her voice to be heard over the waterfall's noise.

"Shhh!" Carina urged, joining her and adding, more quietly, "It's possible someone heard us talking the last time we came here, and that's what alerted the men."

"I very much doubt anyone can hear us over that thing." Parthenia nodded at the towering cascade. "Shall we explore further? I'd love to know what's through there." She indicated the opening where the men had been standing.

"Me too, but we have to be careful." Parthenia's breeziness was making Carina uneasy.

They skirted the perimeter of the wide pool. Translucent crustaceans crawled in the clear water of the shallows. The central area was obscured by mist.

"I have to admit," Parthenia commented, "this does remind me strongly of the mountain castle on Ostillon."

"Feeling more persuaded I'm right?"

"I never said you were wrong, but I know how much this means to you. It's easy to see evidence for something when you want it to be true."

They'd reached the exit. Her pulse quickening, Carina signaled Parthenia to stay back. She drew her gun and peered out. A passageway crossed the exit traveling in two directions. It was empty.

"Left or right?" Parthenia asked.

The right-hand path sloped upward. On Ostillon, the mages had placed their documents in the highest part of the castle, in an open-air chamber that commanded a view of the surrounding lands. Had the mages who had fled Earth left something behind to tell their story?

"This way," said Carina, turning right. She walked a little ahead of her sister, one hand on her elixir canister, the other carrying her sidearm. Parthenia had drawn hers too.

As before, openings led from the passage. Some revealed dusty, bare rooms, others were the beginnings of more passages. If there had ever been doors to the entrances they'd long since rotted away. A deep silence pressed in on Carina's ears, broken only by their soft footfalls. She almost began to believe the men had been figments of her imagination, but Oriana and Ferne had seen them too.

Why hadn't they arrived this time? Had Transporting into the cave and avoiding the outer entrance really foiled them?

"What's that?" Parthenia asked.

"What?"

"That, on the floor. Be careful!"

Carina looked down just in time to see an irregularity in the dust-covered ground as she trod on it. She barely registered the faint striations in the uniform surface before a click sounded and the rattle of heavy chains burst out. A metal cage slammed down.

Parthenia screamed.

The edge of the cage had hit her feet. She collapsed, gasping, outside the cage, but the weight of the heavy metal pinned her. Blood oozed from her shoes.

Carina was trapped inside. Her first instinct was to seize the bars and attempt to lift it. She couldn't move it a centimeter. She began to come to her senses. She took out her elixir canister to Transport them both out of here, back to the shuttle. Then she could Heal Parthenia.

"Ha!" a voice said. "We knew you would be back. Can't resist the place, huh?"

Carina turned. A tall figure was striding toward her—a female figure, but her stature was more like a man's. Had this been one of the people Carina had seen before, mistaking her as male? She was the size of Van Hasty and Pamuk.

Now wasn't the time to find out. Carina lifted her canister to her lips. But before she could drink, she froze. As the woman had walked closer, her face had been revealed in the half light. Carina's grip tightened on her container.

"No need for that," the woman said. "Why don't you stay here a while?" She closed her eyes. She was about to Cast. She must have drunk elixir before announcing her presence.

Parthenia's whimpers were another distraction. Fighting her shock, Carina forced a mouthful of elixir down. It was a matter of who could Cast faster. The woman had a head start on her. Should she Cast Repulse and block whatever the stranger planned to do with them? Or should she go straight to Transport to take them away from danger?

She had a better idea.

She took out her gun and fired.

SHE WAS STANDING in grass in sunshine. Parthenia lay on the ground, rolling in agony, her feet crushed and bloody. Carina fell to her knees. "I'm here, sweetheart. Just a moment." She placed a hand on her poor sister's ankles and Cast Heal, praying the elixir she'd swallowed a few seconds ago remained effective.

Gradually, Parthenia's moans faded. She relaxed onto her back and lifted a hand to her forehead. "That was *awful*."

"Are you sure you're better? Can I take off your shoes and check?" Irrational though it was, she wanted to reassure herself the Cast had worked.

"Be my guest." Parthenia sat up and inspected the damage. "Ugh, they're ruined. I only printed them yesterday."

The shoes were soaked in blood. Carina carefully slipped them off. "You Transported us out? I don't know how you managed it."

"It was hard to concentrate but I thought you would have your hands full. It never occurred to me the place might be booby-trapped."

"Me neither." She removed Parthenia's blood-encrusted socks. Her feet were whole and unmarked. Carina took a deep breath and exhaled. "You're fine."

"I know." Parthenia patted her arm. "You can relax. It was a good idea to shoot that woman. A pulse round is always faster than a Cast. Did you get a chance to see if you hit her before you were Transported?"

"No, but if it wasn't a kill shot she'll just Heal herself—or get someone else to do it for her. Did you notice anyone else?"

"It was as much as I could do to Cast, dear. I wasn't making detailed observations."

Carina chuckled. "Sorry." She took in their surroundings. Parthenia had Transported them to within a short distance of the shuttle, where Hsiao and Darius waited. Though she didn't like the idea, they'd been forced to bring their youngest brother along to Cloak the shuttle on their journey to Earth. "We should get back to the shuttle." She began to put her sister's socks on but Parthenia told her she would wear the shoes with bare feet.

They began the short walk, Parthenia padding gingerly in her wet shoes.

"There was no warning from Darius this time," Carina said. "The woman must have arrived after I triggered the trap. Did you..." she hesitated "...did you get a good look at her?"

"From my position on the floor, looking past you while enduring unbearable pain? Not a *very* good look, no."

"So you didn't see her face?"

"Carina, what are you trying to say?"

"She...uhh...you're going to find this hard to believe. Do you at least believe me now about the men I saw, and that one of them was Casting?"

"I do. I admit you must have been correct. What new revelation do you have for me?"

"The woman—she might have been as burly as a female Black Dog, but she...she looked like Ma."

Parthenia halted. "Are you sure?"

"It isn't the kind of mistake that's easy to make."

"But you were freaked out, and you must have been thinking about mages and our history and so on. Maybe—"

"She had Ma's face. She looked even more like her than you or me. I'm not wrong, and," she added with some heat "I'd appreciate it if you would stop dissing everything I say."

"I'm sorry, but I don't understand how that's possible."

"It isn't. Not any way I can think of. But it's true."

17

They were nearly at the shuttle—Carina thought she could see its faint outlines under the camouflage sheet—but there was no sign of Darius or Hsiao. Parthenia was peering around in a confused way too, and she opened her mouth as if to call out, but Carina put a hand on her arm, silencing her.

Something wasn't right.

She stepped off the track, taking her sister with her, and crouched in the undergrowth.

Parthenia did the same, whispering. "What's wrong?"

"I don't know."

If the pilot and their brother were in trouble, Darius would have Sent a message.

"They might have gone for a walk," said Parthenia softly. "It must be boring waiting for us with nothing to do."

Carina couldn't explain her feeling, so she just gave a shake of her head. She took out her elixir and swigged a little. *Darius, where are you? Is everything okay?*

Carina. Thank the stars. They took my elixir. They knew exactly what they were—

The sudden cut off in his reply sent a shockwave of alarm through her body.

Darius! Darius!

Parthenia grabbed her arm. "What's wrong? Has something happened to them?"

Sorry, Darius Sent, *They're hurting Hsiao, trying to make her tell them where the shuttle is. Please help, Carina. I can't do anything without my elixir.*

Where are you?

His description wasn't helpful. He and Hsiao had gone for a walk, as Parthenia guessed. All he could say was they'd walked roughly south for about fifteen minutes, and they were surrounded by trees— exactly like everywhere in this place.

If it were only a matter of Transporting Darius out of danger, she could have done it. She had a fix on him. But not Hsiao. She couldn't Transport the pilot unless she could see her, and it sounded as though hostiles were in close contact. She definitely didn't want to take any of them along by accident.

Hold on, she Sent. *We'll be there as fast as we can.*

"What's happening?!" Parthenia demanded as Carina opened her eyes.

"Someone's got them." She peered out, checking for movement, but the forest was still. She slowly rose to her feet.

Parthenia also stood up. "Who?"

"No idea. But whoever it is, they know all about mages. They took Darius's elixir off him. And they know about the shuttle, but they don't know where it is." She left out the part about the attackers torturing Hsiao. "I only know roughly where they are. We can Transport some of the way, but we'll have to be very careful. The woods must be crawling with people looking for us."

"You think the woman we saw in the caves is connected to this?"

"She has to be. It's all connected. Are you ready?"

Parthenia nodded and grasped her arm again.

"Take your gun out."

"What?"

"We have to be ready for anything."

With a look of distaste, her sister drew out her sidearm.

Before Transporting them, Carina checked the level of elixir in her canister. There was plenty but, as always, her supply was finite.

They appeared in a patch of open ground, a glade, surrounded by trees. Instantly, they sank down. The sunlight was warm on their backs and insects buzzed and crawled in the grass.

"I can't hear anything," Parthenia whispered. "Can you?"

Aside from birdsong and insect noise, their surroundings were quiet...except... Carina strained her ears. "I can hear them."

Easing through the undergrowth softly, she led Parthenia toward the faint sounds of voices. One was deep, demanding, and insistent. The other was shrill with pain and fear. She couldn't make out what they were saying, but she was in no doubt that the higher voice was Hsiao's and the other was her interrogator's. She hoped the pilot would resist a little longer. If the enemy found the shuttle it would make escape trickier.

Parthenia hissed, "I can see them."

An arching, thorny stem had snagged Carina's pants. She put away her gun to carefully detach the stem before looking in the direction her sister had indicated. In between the tree trunks in the distance was a group of figures. She made out ten or eleven gathered into a circle, facing inward.

Shit.

Hsiao and Darius would be in the center, the objects of attention. If she could only see Hsiao she could extract her, but the men and women blocked her view. "We have to get closer." She took out her weapon and they crept on. Then she halted. "Wait a minute." She sank to her haunches, pulling Parthenia down with her, then swigged elixir and Cast. *Darius, we know where you are but I need a line of sight to Hsiao. Can you do something?*

I'll try.

Thanks. Be careful.

"Carina," whispered Parthenia, her tone strained. "I think we've been spotted."

As she spoke, the cracking of twigs and rustle of bodies forcing a path through vegetation burst from the rear. Only fifty or so meters distant, men were heading their way.

Carina leapt up. "Run!"

They sped toward Hsiao and Darius. Keeping her focus on the group, she zigzagged through the forest, hoping to reduce her chances of being hit. Sure enough, pulse rounds hit the trees to each side, searing and scorching the bark. The scent of burning wood filled the air along with the snap and crackle of flames.

The people holding Darius and Hsiao seemed to have noticed what was happening. Pulses began to fly from that direction too. She was running from danger into danger. Where was Parthenia?

Shouting erupted from the captors. There was a scuffle going on. Darius had to be creating a distraction. The group was breaking apart. She caught a glimpse of Hsiao, and her heart lurched. The pilot was on her knees. Her hair glinted with wetness. Blood?

She could get her out. She had to get her out. But she needed a few seconds to make the Cast—a few seconds she didn't have. The minute she stopped running and dodging she would be shot or captured.

Suddenly, from nowhere, Parthenia was at her side. "Do it! I'll cover you."

They stopped near a bunch of ferns. Carina crouched down. Through the leafy stalks she could just make out Hsiao. Darius seemed to be struggling with two men. The other hostiles had spread out and were heading their way. A pulse grazed the ferns, setting them alight.

Parthenia was firing, sweeping her weapon to the front and back. "Hurry!"

Checking Hsiao's position again, she drank elixir and closed her eyes. Her sister's panting breaths sounded in her ears. Heat glowed on her cheek. The fire in the fern was spreading. A shriek came from somewhere close by. *Hsiao.*

She Cast.

Hard deck was under her knees. The noise and heat were gone. "Hsiao?!"

The pilot was curled on her side, holding her head, moaning. Her face was a mask of blood, dripping from cuts on her scalp, but she was alive.

Darius was also here in the shuttle passenger cabin but so were the men holding him. They stared wildly, their mouths gaping. Carina strode the two short steps required to reach them and shot two in the head. The third had time to raise his hands and mutter a plea before she shot him too. The awful scent of burned human flesh oozed from the bodies.

"You probably didn't have to kill them," Parthenia protested.

Always the pacifist, she'd turned soft over their long voyage.

"I think I *probably* did," Carina retorted. "Have you seen what they did to Hsiao?"

Darius dropped to the pilot's side. "Someone give me elixir, please!"

"Thank the stars it's all over," said Parthenia, handing him her canister.

"I told them," groaned Hsiao. "I told them. I'm sorry."

"You told them where the shuttle is?" Carina asked.

The pilot couldn't answer, only grimace and nod.

"I'll Heal her," Darius said, "and we can fly out."

Carina darted into the pilot's cabin and checked the sensors. People were moving toward the vessel. A few minutes ago the woods in this area had been empty. Had the people been Transported here? She started up the engine.

"What are you doing?" Parthenia asked from the doorway.

"What does it look like?"

"But we haven't removed the camouflage sheet."

"No time." She jabbed a finger at the approaching figures.

"Can you fly it?"

"It's been a while but I'll have to try. Tell Darius to Cloak us as soon as he's finished Healing Hsiao. And you all need to strap in."

Parthenia disappeared.

Carina gave a command and her seat harness snaked over her, closing with a click. After setting the coordinates, she grabbed the controls and guided the shuttle upward. Resistance from the sheet registered on the display. She ignored it. Outside, the vessel would be rearing up from among the trees, ripping the cover from the ground, and the whine of her engine would reverberate through the forest.

An alarm sounded and the pilot's interface blinked. They were being fired upon, but she doubted the enemy carried more than small arms. As soon as Darius Cast Cloak, they would be invisible to their attackers anyway.

While she flew them away, more pressing problems bothered her. Who was the woman in the caves and why did she look like Ma? And how had someone guessed there would be a starship shuttle waiting for them in the woods?

18

Bryce was in the shuttle bay. Reading her expression as she descended from the shuttle, he said, "Another bad trip?"

"You know that saying about the third try being the lucky one?"

"Er...third time lucky?"

"That's it. It isn't true."

"At least you all got back in one piece. That's the main thing."

Darius, Parthenia, and Hsiao were heading for the exit.

"Hey," Carina called after them, "see you in the mission room in fifteen minutes for debriefing."

No one replied as they left.

"That's a bit harsh," said Bryce. "Maybe you should give them more time to rest."

"Time is exactly what we're running out of. The Dogs gave me a week to figure this out before they take matters into their own hands, and we're one day down already. If they're let loose on Earth with no prep can you imagine the carnage? Honestly, I don't care if they screw things up for themselves. That's on them. They're big enough and ugly enough to run their own lives. But I don't want them to ruin our chances of living peacefully and openly."

"What happened down there? You sound desperate."

"Ugh..." She put a hand to her forehead. Where to begin? Before she could explain, a woman dashed into the bay—the last person she wanted to talk to right now, or ever.

"There you are!" Cheepy announced in a triumphant tone. "How come I haven't seen you since I came out of Deep Sleep? You've been avoiding me, right? I suspected you were hogging Earth all to yourself, and it's true. How many times have you been planetside now?" She got up close to Carina's face. "How many?!"

Hogging Earth to myself? "I'm glad to see you're over the effects of stasis. Things on the surface are tricky at the mo—"

"Don't give me that bullshit. You want to be the only person who gets to go down there and have all the fun. You, your family, and your cronies." She gave Bryce a look of disgust. "I won't stand for it. I never wanted to come on this stupid voyage in the first place. You tricked me into it, taking me away from everything I knew and everyone I loved."

"We've discussed this a million times," Carina said between her teeth. "You were the one who wanted to leave Sot Loza. It isn't my fault you changed your mind at the last second. And if you'd stayed, there's a good chance you would be dead by now. So you should really be thanking me."

"*Thanking you!* That's rich. You consigned me to living with thugs and weirdos, and I should thank you?!"

It had been a long, harrowing day. Something snapped. "Do you think I *want* you here, you nasty, whiny, stuck-up b—"

"Let's go," Bryce interrupted. "Gotta do that debriefing, remember?"

Cheepy's glare followed them out of the bay. If she'd been even remotely intelligent, Carina would have been worried about leaving her alone with the shuttle. She was sufficiently stupid to try to fly herself to Earth in it. However, she didn't possess anywhere near the smarts to even start the engines. The worst she could do was injure herself trying, and Carina secretly hoped she did.

"Am I a thug, a weirdo, or a crony?" Bryce asked as they walked down the passageway.

"All three, and an adorable thug, weirdo, and crony too."

On the way to the mission room they encountered Chi-tang, who was creeping about surreptitiously, peering over his shoulder.

"She's in the bay," Carina told him.

"Uhh, thanks." Chi-tang headed in the opposite direction.

VAN HASTY and Jackson had invited themselves to the debriefing. Carina eyed them as they came in and sat down. She didn't say anything. She had to concede they had a right to attend. "I want Officer Matt here too. Is he still in the brig? And what about Nahla?"

"She's on her way," Parthenia replied, "along with Ferne and Oriana."

Another attendee had appeared: Ava. "I heard you're going to talk about Earth. Is it okay if I listen?"

"Of course," replied Carina, mentally chastising herself for forgetting about the Marchonish women. They were so meek and mild, so self-effacing, forgetting them was easy. Ava was the most outspoken of the bunch, but that wasn't saying a lot.

Jackson comm'd the brig guard to bring Matt, and everyone waited. Nahla came in with the twins. Lastly, the man from Earth arrived, wearing handcuffs.

"I don't think those are necessary," Carina said to his guard, nodding at the cuffs. What exactly would Matt do in a room full of mercenaries and mages, and if he escaped, where would he run to?

The guard unlocked the restraints. Jackson told him he would comm when it was time for the prisoner to return to the brig.

"Do you really need to keep him confined?" Ava asked. "I'm sure he won't do any harm."

"That's just your opinion," Jackson growled.

"And I'm entitled to it," Ava retorted, her eyes narrowing, "as his medic."

"I won't do anything," said Matt. "I promise. Anyway, I haven't done anything wrong. You don't have any right to lock me up."

Carina huffed in exasperation. "Oh, give him a cabin, for star's sake. We have more important problems than a deluded Earthman wandering around the ship."

"*I'm* the deluded one?" Matt gave a slight shake of his head. "I don't think so, though I have to admit, the effort you guys have put into this is impressive. You've learned a whole new language, built this fake ship, printed strange clothes... You've invented an entire history for yourselves too. You know, if you worked as hard at something else —a career, for instance, or a business—you could go far."

"What's he blathering on about, Lin?" Jackson snapped.

Putting her face in her hands, Carina wondered if they should take Matt's translator and only return it when they were ready to speak to him.

Bryce patted her back. "Shall we start?"

Darius spoke first, explaining what had happened to him and Hsiao. His report was simple and didn't contain much more information than Carina already knew. He and the pilot had gone for a walk, imagining the woods were empty. They'd *seemed* empty, until the men had pounced on them and, before Darius had a chance to Cast, they'd snatched his elixir canister. Then Hsiao's torture had commenced. Why no one had hurt Darius, who also knew the shuttle's location, hadn't been revealed.

Parthenia then told the story of what had happened in the caves. The time line of events showed that Darius and Hsiao had been attacked only minutes after the cage had slammed down over Carina. The connection was clear.

"So after I sprung the trap," Carina said, "someone sent—probably Transported—a team to the forest to find a starship shuttle. They knew that was how we arrived. Darius, did you get a bad feeling about a presence in the mountain like you did before?"

"I didn't, but I was distracted by the attack on Hsiao and me."

"They wanted to prevent us from returning to the ship," said Parthenia. "They wanted to cut off our avenue of escape and keep us on Earth."

Carina took in a breath. "There's something else to tell you. Parthenia can't confirm it because she didn't have a clear view, so you only have my word, but..." she focused on her siblings "...I'm absolutely certain the woman in the caves looked like Ma."

"She looked like Mother?" Oriana repeated. "How?"

"She just did. I can't explain it any better than you."

Jackson said, "You all look kinda alike, and you said the woman was a mage. It isn't that strange, is it?"

"There are thousands of mages," Parthenia snapped. "Probably tens of thousands, who look nothing like each other. Jace didn't look like us, did he?"

"Fair point," Jackson conceded.

"What does it mean?" Oriana asked, with a troubled expression.

"I don't know," Carina replied. In truth, on the shuttle ride back to the ship she'd formed a suspicion, but she didn't want to air it, not without more proof. Her idea was outlandish and she would sound unhinged, yet it was the only possible explanation.

She turned to Matt. "Have you followed everything so far?"

"I understand what you've said. Whether I believe it..."

"Whether you believe it or not doesn't really matter. Just imagine that what we've been saying is true. Have you ever heard of anyone who can do the things me and my family can—Transporting to locations and Healing injuries, for instance?"

"Never. Or, at least, not outside children's stories and vid dramas."

"Is it possible you just don't know about it?"

"No way. Something like that would be big news."

Parthenia said, "So mages on Earth are living in secret, the same as everywhere else. Disappointing, but perhaps to be expected."

Carina couldn't deny it.

"The situation is worse than that," said Nahla. "Not only do mages live in fear of persecution on Earth, a set of them are waiting for others to arrive from space, and whatever they intend, it isn't good. You don't trap people in cages or torture them to be friendly."

"They knew we would go there," Carina said. "They know the mountain hideaway is the only place returning mages could go if they wanted to connect with the past."

"I discovered something that might be relevant," Nahla announced. "Fifty-three years ago, the media reported that a starship had arrived from outer space and was in orbit around the planet. The reports were quickly discredited and, from what I can tell, most were deleted. I only found a few, hidden deep in the archives."

"So some other mages made it back before us," said Ferne. "The group in the caves must have attacked them too."

"And had all news of them removed from public view," Oriana added.

"There's no reason to think they were mages," Parthenia countered. "They could have been any returning colonists. Perhaps there's a conspiracy to keep Earth natives ignorant of the possibility of human life existing on other planets. Perhaps the information about the departure of colony ships wasn't lost, but is a deliberate attempt to erase history."

Carina said, "But why would the authorities not want anyone to know about people leaving the planet in the past? Matt, what's the general opinion about the possibility of colonizing other worlds? Is it something people talk about?"

"Not seriously. If there are other habitable planets out there, they're so far away it would take several lifetimes to reach them. A space journey that long isn't practical."

"You've never heard of Deep Sleep?" Carina asked. "I mean, putting people into a state of stasis for years at a time, where they're only just alive?"

"Sounds like science fiction."

"The tech has been forgotten," said Nahla, "along with starship engine drives. No one on Earth could build a colony ship even if they wanted to. But the impression I get is that there isn't much interest. Earth people are content with their living conditions, and it isn't hard to see why. It's a peaceful place with little hardship. Most of the population lives a long, happy life."

"Sounds idyllic," said Oriana.

"It isn't idyllic if you have to hide an important part of yourself," said Carina.

Van Hasty spoke for the first time. "I've listened enough. Me and Jackson came here to find out if there's a reason the Dogs can't go planetside, and all we've heard is mages this, mages that. You've got no reason to keep us here except that our arrival might upset your little plan to live happily ever after doing your magic tricks whenever you feel like it."

"I have to say," Ava interjected softly, "I agree. My friends and I have waited years to reach a place we can finally call home. Many of us are in relationships. All we want to do is to settle down and raise children, and Earth sounds ideal."

Though Van Hasty and Ava spoke separately they voiced the sentiment from the non-mage contingent aboard ship. Lines between the mercenaries and the Marchonish women had become blurred over the years as they'd fallen in love and formed partnerships. Carina's heart was heavy as she responded, "That isn't unreasonable. I want the same for my family. I'm just asking for a little time."

Van Hasty stood up. "What you want could take an eternity. You've got six days, Lin. Come on, Jackson."

The mercs departed.

"I'll go too," Ava said. "Unless there's something else I should know?"

Carina shook her head.

"Matt, come with me. I'll find a cabin for you."

Only Carina, her siblings, and Bryce remained in the mission room. No one spoke. What was there to say? They faced a problem that could take years to solve, and they had mages actively working against them.

The only thing she knew for sure was that however they tackled their anonymous enemies it had to be done in secret. Any whisper of a violent conflict related to their kind would tarnish their reputation forever among the ordinary, peaceful people of Earth, destroying the chance of mages ever living openly.

19

Regardless of the urgency of the situation, Carina had to sleep. After a quick dinner she went with Bryce to their cabin and got ready for bed.

As soon as they were under the covers Bryce wrapped his arms around her. "Try not to worry too much. We'll figure things out. We've got through worse things than this."

"I know, but—"

"And we've made it this far. If it wasn't for your determination we could never have done it. You should be proud."

"Yeah, but—"

"Go to sleep."

He knew her well.

He added, "Unless you want to...?"

"Too tired, sorry."

"Sure." He snuggled closer.

Warm and secure, her weariness overcame her anxiety and she drifted off.

Hours later, something woke her. She wasn't sure what. Bryce was lying on his back, quietly snoring. It couldn't have been that. She was well-used to his sleeping habits, as no doubt he was to hers.

A tiny light overhead gave the cabin minimal illumination, just enough to avoid utter darkness. Bryce's bare chest rose and fell. She laid a hand on it, appreciating the familiar sensation. At the meeting, Ava had mentioned the wish of the couples aboard to settle on Earth and raise families. Bryce had voiced the possibility for them, too, a long time ago. Though their experiences on Sot Loza had dissuaded him of the urgency, she hadn't forgotten the suggestion.

She had no practical objection. The only problem was, the odds of their offspring being mages was fifty-fifty, and she didn't want to bring a child into the world where they might be feared and hated, perhaps exploited. She would never forget the life Ma had endured. Creating a new person, knowing that a similar life for them was a risk—no matter how remote—was something she could never do.

But that didn't mean she and Bryce couldn't be happy. Over the course of the voyage her feelings for him had deepened and she was in no doubt that at the Matching on Pirine, when mages had the opportunity to find their life partners, she'd made the right choice.

Raising herself up on one elbow, she leaned over to kiss his lips. It took him a moment to wake up and when he did he was a little startled until he realized what was going on. Then he returned her kiss.

She said, "I'm not so tired now."

He smiled and turned onto his side, taking her into his arms. They kissed again.

Her ear comm chirruped.

"Shit." She reached for the side table, where it lay, and popped it into her ear. "Yeah?"

"Get to the bridge, Lin," Jackson said. "You want to see this."

"It's Jackson," she told Bryce. "Something's up. You should come too."

After hastily pulling on some clothes, they jogged through the passageways. Jackson didn't provide any updates along the way, so she guessed whatever the issue was it couldn't be that urgent. What she saw as she walked onto the bridge contradicted her assumption. "What the hell?!"

In the center of the bridge hung a holo, representing what she assumed was readings from the short-range scanners. Somewhere near the *Bathsheba* was a space-faring vessel. She didn't recognize the type but it wasn't much bigger than a regular shuttle.

"How long has *that* been here?"

"Only a few minutes," Jackson replied. "Comms has been trying to hail her, but no luck so far."

The comms officer was speaking into her mic. She looked over and gave a slight shake of her head.

"Keep trying," Carina ordered.

"It has to be from Earth," said Bryce.

"Well, duh," said Van Hasty. "Unless you know of another inhabited planet in this system."

"No need to guess how they found us either," Carina said. *Dammit. I was so busy worrying about our problems I didn't think about the repercussions of what happened today. If the hostile mages know we arrived from space, they know there's a colony ship somewhere close by.*"

Van Hasty added, "And the obvious place to hide around here is behind this big ol' satellite."

"Now they found us," Jackson said, "what do we do about it? If they didn't mean nasty business they would answer our hail. Is it time to turn on the Obliterator?"

"That old thing?" Van Hasty scoffed. "We haven't used it in years. Someone will have to dust off the cobwebs or it might blow *us* up instead."

"Sounds like a job for Chi-tang."

"Uh-uh." Van Hasty shook her head emphatically. "That's a negative. If we get him in here his goddamned loud-mouthed girlfriend's gonna follow him in."

The irony of the burly female merc calling Cheepy loud-mouthed wasn't lost on Carina, but she kept her opinion to herself. "Do we know if it's carrying weapons?" She studied the holo but it was hard to tell what might be armaments.

Jackson replied, "If she is, she hasn't used them." He checked his console. "Scanners aren't detecting anything powering up."

"It would take balls to fire on a ship a hundred times the size of your own," Bryce commented.

"If their mission isn't offensive," said Carina, "and they don't want to talk, they're here for surveillance. They want to know what they're up against. While we've been chatting they've been taking readings, finding out as much as they can about us. Let's not give them the luxury."

"I'll comm Chi-tang," Jackson said.

"No, wait." She chewed the side of her thumb. The *Bathsheba* could easily destroy the little vessel, providing her captain was stupid enough to stick around while the Obliterator built energy. But there was the need for secrecy to consider. Astronomy might no longer be of much interest to people on Earth, but there had to be a few die-hards with telescopes who wouldn't fail to notice a sudden massive burst of power on the far side of the moon. Keeping a violent conflict hidden from Earth eyes was paramount.

Besides, there was another good reason to not destroy the enemy vessel.

"I don't want to annihilate the ship," she said, "just scare it off."

"We can do that easily," said Jackson. "We can fire this bird's pulse cannon across her bows. That should give them the willies."

"Yeah," Carina agreed. "Do it." She sat down, keeping her gaze focused on the holo image.

"If the pulse cannon don't do the trick firing up the Obliterator will," Bryce said reassuringly, taking the adjacent seat.

The cannon fired. Streaks of light streamed above and below the enemy vessel. There was no need for a repeat of the warning. Her thrusters spurted and she slipped from sight, disappearing over the moon's rocky horizon.

"I dunno," Van Hasty said ruefully. "Maybe we should have destroyed that ship while we could. They can't have many space-worthy craft, and we don't want them to think we're pussies."

"They don't need spacecraft," Carina replied. "They must know the reason we came all this way is because we want to settle on Earth, so winning a space battle isn't important. The battle for what we want is going to take place on the surface. Blowing their ship up wouldn't have made any difference. They wouldn't risk putting anyone important in danger. But this way..." she got to her feet and opened a screen "...we can read her trace."

Jackson laughed. "And find out where she goes. You always were a smarty-pants, Carina Lin."

"Too smart for her own good," said Van Hasty. "Six days."

20

T
he shuttle swept low over a vast tree canopy, stretching to the horizon on every side. Blazing sunlight glinted from every leaf under an azure sky.

"*This* is where the vessel landed?" asked Bryce.

He was crowded into the pilot's cabin with Carina and Parthenia, who had insisted on returning to the surface despite Carina's protests.

"Somewhere hereabouts," Bibik replied, nodding toward an undefined spot a few hundred meters below.

Carina decided to voice the obvious question. "But how?"

Bibik shrugged. "That's for you guys to figure out. Just let me know where to set this bird down."

That was another unanswerable question.

"Do another circuit," Carina replied. "We need some time to think about it."

They returned to the passenger cabin.

"Maybe the scan data is wrong," said Parthenia. "We should comm the ship and get someone to check it."

"I checked it twice already." Carina slumped into a seat. "I wouldn't bring us all this way without confirming it. This is where the spy ship landed."

"Maybe they have a special Cast that allows them to dissolve trees," Bryce said.

"And regrow them in a day?" asked Carina. "That isn't what's happened, believe me. I have an idea what it is, but I don't know what we can do about it."

"It's Semblance, right?" asked Darius.

"Yes!" Parthenia exclaimed. "That's it! It has to be."

"Semblance?" Bryce frowned. "That's a new one, to me at least."

"No, it isn't," said Carina. "You remember the Dirksen headquarters on Ostillon, in the mountains?"

"Oh, yeah. The entrance was fake."

"We encountered the same Cast on Magog. The boundary of the Dark Mage's estate was false. You could step through it and see the real boundary, the same as we stepped through the rock into the mountain castle. Semblance creates an illusion mirroring something nearby."

"I get it now. The trees aren't real. They're obscuring a shuttle landing site."

"It doesn't really help, though, does it?" Parthenia asked.

Carina replied, "At least we've confirmed this is mage work—ancient mage work. I didn't know about Semblance until we encountered the mountain castle, and I didn't have a name for it until we met the Dark Mage, Wei, on Magog. My grandmother never taught me the Cast, and Ma didn't teach it to her kids. So I guess it must have been forgotten by the mages in our sector."

Darius said, "I wonder what other Casts Earth Mages can do that we can't?"

"Who knows?" asked Parthenia. "Not too many, I hope. But, to return to my point, knowing that the shuttle landing site is there even though we can't see it isn't helpful. Even if we could figure out exactly where it is, we can't land there ourselves. Assuming Bibik could set us down in an open spot, Darius can't keep our shuttle Cloaked forever."

Bryce groaned. "You mean we have to trek in? How far? Conditions down there must be shit."

"And there will be snakes and spiders," Parthenia added. "But I don't see a way around it."

"It isn't as bad as it looks," said Carina. "We can Transport part of the way. If we can't see the landing site we have the rough coordinates from the trace data. I'll ask Bibik to find the closest place to land, then we'll take it from there."

She returned to the pilot's cabin to speak to him, but deeper problems were bothering her, problems she wanted to understand better before she mentioned them to the others. Why had the people who had spied on them constructed a secret base deep within a jungle and obscured it with Semblance?

Nahla had scoured Earth's news media reports and found no mention of a spacecraft visiting the Moon and returning, yet surely it must have been noticed, if only by people who watched the skies as a hobby. Somehow, these people were being silenced. So the base was hidden from regular view and whoever was running it had influence within the highest level of Earth governments.

Why go to all this trouble to keep their activities secret, and how were they managing it?

Something nefarious was going on, and it didn't only involve mages.

PARTHENIA AND BIBIK were taking a while to say goodbye before the party set off to find the shuttle landing site. Carina waited patiently. The two had been serious for a couple of years, and after what had happened to Hsiao it was natural that Parthenia would be concerned about leaving her partner alone, tens of kilometers from help on Earth and hundreds of klicks from his merc buddies on the *Bathsheba*. He wasn't a mage so he couldn't Send if he needed them, and they couldn't be sure their comm would work over the distance.

"It was nice of Bibik to volunteer to bring us down," Bryce commented as they waited.

"I think he felt obliged," Carina replied. "Hsiao would have done it but it wouldn't be right for her to take all the risks."

Darius said, "I could stay with him if that would be best. I don't mind."

Carina shook her head. "We need you too." *More than you know.*

The area nearest to their anonymous enemy's base sufficiently open to land the shuttle was a sandy beach at the edge of the jungle. The place was utterly deserted. No signs of human habitations or activity were visible. Though it was conceivable people lived within the jungle bordering the ocean, they couldn't be technologically advanced and so it was unlikely they posed a threat.

They waited in silence as the waves rose and fell and the steady sea breeze ruffled the palm tree leaves. From somewhere in the forest came the shrill cry of a bird.

Parthenia emerged from beneath the shuttle's new camouflage sheet, which mimicked the edge of the shoreline. She looked as though she'd been crying, but her expression became neutral as she walked over, trudging through the loose sand.

Darius put a hand on her shoulder. "I'm sure he'll be fine. We're in the middle of nowhere, and no one will have spotted where we landed. I was Cloaking the ship. They didn't know where it was on our last trip."

She stiffened. Brushing her hair from her eyes and ignoring her brother's reassurances, she asked, "Are we Transporting directly there? No stops?"

"I don't see any point," Carina replied. "It's a long way, but I'm sure Darius can manage it." Looking at her brother, she added, "Right?"

"I can do it, but how close do we want to be? They might be expecting us."

"Hmm. You're right. They might have guessed we would track their ship's trace. In case they've posted lookouts, shall we say one K out? We can check things out as we get closer and reassess." She scanned the others' faces for approval.

Bryce grimaced but said nothing.

Darius made his Cast, and they appeared on a raised portion of ground, thick tree trunks surrounding them. They seemed to be alone. Unfortunately, the high elevation didn't give them a good vantage point. All that could be seen was ranks of trees hung with vines and moss descending down the slope. The line where reality ended and the Semblance began was impossible to spot.

The humidity was stifling. Carina was instantly coated in sweat, and the local insect life had discovered them almost as quickly. A flying creature alighted on the back of her hand and began to probe with its proboscis. She killed it with a slap.

"Anyone know a Protect Against Bloodsuckers Cast?" Bryce asked hopefully.

"Sorry, but no," Darius replied. "I could try to invent one but it would take me a while."

"Another time." Bryce took out an interface from his backpack, consulted it, and pointed. "The shuttle landing site is that way."

"Should I Cloak us?" asked Darius.

"Save it for when we really need it," Carina replied. "I think we're okay for now."

"We waited too long on our first mission to Earth," Parthenia countered. "Maybe it would be a good idea to use it pre-emptively."

"We have quite a walk ahead of us over rough terrain. If Darius Cloaks us the entire way he'll use up his elixir supply."

Parthenia shrugged. "I'm just saying, we might not have been captured on our first mission if—"

"I hear you. We'll Cloak when we're two hundred meters out or if we spot anyone."

They set off down the slope.

After five minutes of battling invertebrates literally after their blood while also slithering down the leaf mold and loose soil, clinging to plant stems and draping vines for support, Carina cursed. "Why the hell did they build a freaking shuttle landing site out here?"

Bryce asked, "You mean why not somewhere more convenient, like an air-conditioned shopping mall?"

"That's exactly what I mean."

"We could browse the latest fashions while fighting our enemies," said Darius. "Ferne and Oriana would be totally on board with that."

Parthenia murmured, "I hope Bibik is all right."

As they reached the lower ground the insect life increased. A black cloud descended, and soon every square centimeter of open skin was under attack. Carina pulled her shirt sleeves over her hands and the hood of her jacket over her head, but her efforts barely helped.

"This is impossible," Bryce complained, running his hands over his face.

"I agree," said Parthenia. "We can't deal with this any longer. We simply have to Transport closer."

Carina couldn't argue. "Darius, can you Cloak us and then put us a hundred meters from the coordinates?"

The insects were gone and so was the humidity. Cool, dry air sucked the sweat from her skin. She lowered her hood. The same deep blue sky she'd glimpsed in gaps in the canopy still hung overhead, but the view had altered in every other way. Where there had once been deep brown forest floor lay an expanse of gray concrete. Towering trees had been replaced by columns of shining steel. The spacecraft that had spied on the *Bathsheba* stood on its pad in the distance, and four similar craft were positioned nearby.

The enemy didn't have just one space-traveling vessel, it had five.

The shock she felt seemed to extend to the others. For several moments, no one spoke.

Then Bryce said, "Well, we found what we were looking for. Now what?"

"I guess we get closer and see what else we can find out," she replied.

"I Cast the Cloak to a diameter of roughly five meters," said Darius. "If anyone steps outside the circle they risk being seen."

Figures moved between the columns and the shuttles. They looked more like techies and mechanics than guards, but Darius's reminder still applied. There was little chance that the sudden appearance of a bunch of insect-bitten strangers would go unnoticed.

"There's some powerful magic going on here," Bryce commented as they walked.

"It isn't magic," Carina replied irritably before asking, "What do you mean?"

"The whole place is air-conditioned and I can't see any barriers. Can you?"

As well as no ceiling visible above, forest fringed the site on every side. Something was confining the controlled atmosphere.

"Can Semblance do this?" Parthenia asked.

Carina didn't know the answer. She hadn't noticed the phenomenon the two previous time she'd encountered the Cast. In a sense, it wasn't important. Generating an illusion this vast was impressive work by itself.

An opening appeared at the base of a column and a four-wheeled vehicle sped out. It was the kind of passenger-carrying automotive she'd noticed as absent from Earth, according to Matt. The top was open and sitting in it were six men in three rows. Only one figure, seated at the front, wasn't in uniform.

"Shit," breathed Bryce.

The man in plain clothes was pointing in their direction.

"Don't worry," Carina said. "He can't possibly see us."

"Are you sure?"

She hesitated. The car was heading their way. She looked over her shoulder. Nothing stood between them and the edge of the site. "I don't *think* so."

Darius was also staring, dumbfounded, at the approaching vehicle. "I definitely Cloaked us."

The lead guard lifted a gun and aimed.

"Maybe you should..." Carina suggested as the vehicle zoomed closer.

"Uh huh." Darius took out his canister.

She put her rifle to her shoulder and stepped in front of her brother.

For some reason, Darius's Cloak didn't seem to be working, and they couldn't run from their attackers. They would never reach the forest in time before being mowed down. All they could hope was that he could Transport them before someone was hit.

The guard fired, and the round narrowly missed Parthenia.

Carina returned fire, winging the man who had shot at them. As he buckled, the vehicle veered, and the men behind him began to shoot. Bryce was firing now and so was Parthenia. Carina pressed the trigger again and a second guard went down.

A shriek.

Parthenia had been hit.

The car was only meters away. The man in front glared and grinned manically as he screamed orders at his men.

Carina's finger froze on her trigger. Her rifle spurted rounds, all going astray.

As she stared at the man, all sound seemed to disappear from the world. Everything zipped from existence until it was only her and the grinning man, alone in the universe, eyes locked.

21

They were back on the beach.

Parthenia was crying out in pain, but she was alive. She rolled on the sand, eyes shut tight, hands clasped to her shoulder. Darius fell to his knees and gulped elixir.

"How did this happen?" Carina wondered aloud. "How the hell could they see us?"

Poor Parthenia. It was the second time she'd been wounded. The Heal Cast would quickly take away her pain but that didn't make the wound hurt less at first. And Hsiao had been attacked too. They were lucky no one had been killed.

Darius had Transported them to a spot at the edge of the waves. A little way along the shore the shuttle stood in the shade of the trees. Bibik would notice them soon and come out to check on Parthenia, no doubt. What to do next? Return to the *Bathsheba*?

She walked to the water's edge and watched the ocean, her mind a blank. She was still coming to grips with her vision of the man riding in the front of the vehicle. The face of the woman in the mountain hideaway flashed up. Suddenly, everything slotted into place.

Bryce joined her and asked quietly, "Is it possible the Cloak Cast didn't work?"

"No way. It's always worked before, and we were standing together. No one should have been able to see us."

"Maybe there's something about that place that makes Casts ineffective. Nice shots back there, by the way."

"Thanks. Target practice helps to pass the time when spending years traveling the galaxy."

"You worked out a lot too as I recall."

He didn't know why, and she'd never told him. It was due to one of the last things Atoi had said before the Regians took her: *You're weak. You can be stronger, and you need to be to protect those brats.*

Bryce's focus had switched from her face to something behind her. "*Damn!*"

"What?"

His eyes narrowed. "Soldiers! Hostiles, in the trees!"

She swiveled. Shapes moved in the undergrowth—men and women in fatigues.

She sipped elixir. There was no time to warn Darius or Parthenia.

A pulse round flashed past and hit a wave, bursting the water into a hissing frenzy. Fighting the urge to run, she closed her eyes and Cast. A second round impacted a wave.

She'd Transported everyone hundreds of meters along the beach. This time they stood at the border of the jungle. Would the soldiers they'd left behind spot the shuttle ? She hoped not, and that Bibik had the good sense to check the area before coming out.

"What was *that* about?" asked Parthenia, putting a hand to her forehead.

"They found us somehow. I had to move us away."

"But how did they know where we were?"

"I don't know. I just had to do something fast."

"You should have Transported us into the shuttle."

"You're right. I didn't have time to think." In truth, she remained dazed with shock. "I'll Transport us there now, and we can get the hell out of here." The mission felt like another failure, despite the revelation that had occurred. If anything, it had only stacked the challenges higher.

"Do they know where the shuttle is?" Parthenia asked, concern edging her tone. "Is that the reason they found us? Has anyone tried to comm Bibik?"

"I haven't," Darius said, "but that can't be why they knew where we were. In the mountains, it was different. There were hardly any places to land a shuttle. They could guess the rough location. But this beach stretches for tens of kilometers."

"I don't believe it!" Bryce exclaimed. "They found us again."

This time, the soldiers were only meters away.

"That's not possible," Carina protested.

The enemy had appeared out of nowhere.

There was no time to Transport.

"Scatter!" she yelled. "Run into the forest! When you get a chance to Cast, rendezvous in the shuttle." She grabbed Bryce's arm. "Stick with me."

By splitting up they would stand a better chance of not being caught, and in the dense forest they might find a spot to hide long enough to Cast, but she couldn't lose Bryce. Alone, he was all but helpless.

She dashed into the trees. Instantly, the undergrowth seemed to grip her, intent on slowing her down. Tree trunks appeared and she raced around them, forcing through ferns and clinging vines, listening for Bryce as he ran behind her. The dreadful humidity descended again and sweat trickled from her face and armpits. Her lungs labored.

Where were the soldiers? Had she escaped them? Her and Bryce's passage through the vegetation would be easy to follow. She could only count on their head start and greater speed to give her the breathing space to Cast.

Casting a glance behind her, she spotted Bryce a few steps to her rear and beyond him approaching soldiers.

She ran on.

Why hadn't the Cloak Cast worked?

How had the soldiers found them twice in a row, in less than a minute? The only way they could be found so easily would be if a mage was Locating them, but that was impossible. He or she would need a personal item, something imbued with their essence, to track them down in that shadowy otherworld only mages could see. Yet they'd left nothing behind on their visits to Earth.

A bamboo thicket rose up, tall and forbidding. The smooth stalks clustered thickly, yet, with a little effort...

"Let's go in here." She eased between the stems, pulling Bryce in after her.

"But we won't be able to move."

"Yes, we will. Better than someone in armor, anyway." She forced a hip into a gap and shouldered the vegetation apart, working her way deeper in. The bamboo was a trap in a sense, but it would give them the time she needed.

In half a minute, they were entirely hidden. She took out her canister.

There was a flash. A soldier had fired at the clump, despite the fact they had no visible target. Smoke billowed up. Leaves at the top of the bamboo stalks turned into flames.

"Carina," Bryce whispered urgently. "You'd better Transport us, fast."

She gulped elixir, but before she Cast, the answer to the puzzle exploded in her mind. She had left things behind in the detention center in Bridgeford. She'd been ordered to remove everything from her pockets, and she'd been carrying items she could use to Locate her brother and sister if they were split up. Someone—she was in no doubt exactly who—had recently gotten hold of her things, and now he could Cast to find her, Parthenia, and Darius at any time.

"Carina!" Bryce urged. "Why are we still here?"

The vegetation crackled as the fire moved closer. Hot air warmed her skin.

"We can't go to the shuttle," she replied. "He'll find us."

"He? Who? Who'll find us?"

She had to warn Parthenia and Darius of the danger. Rather than Transporting, she Sent.

Her sister and brother were disbelieving, but there was no time to argue. She told them her plan. As she finished, she felt Bryce grab her jacket. He thrust her into the bamboo, driving a passage through reluctantly yielding stalks.

The fire had moved closer amazingly fast. A red haze of sparks and flying embers rose behind Bryce. She could smell singed hair. His eyes were wide and desperate as he tried to protect her from the flames.

She drank elixir.

The problem was, she couldn't Transport each of them to two different places at once. Bryce had to return to the shuttle first, and she didn't have time to explain why. As the air became unbearably hot and her chest heaved, she made the Cast.

Bryce was gone.

She'd saved him, or at least delayed his capture.

Now to save herself, and deprive their enemy of his advantage.

The fire was almost upon her.

She gulped elixir, but she choked and the precious fluid erupted from her mouth. She'd dropped her canister. She picked it up and coughed. The smoke made it impossible to breathe.

She had to Cast.

She had to Cast or she would die.

The heat on her skin was unbearable. Her jacket was smoldering.

Lifting her canister to her lips once more, she saw blisters on the backs of her hands. She wouldn't need to close her eyes. They were already swelling shut. She tipped up the container, but only a few drops dribbled into her mouth. The elixir must have spilled out when she dropped it.

The bamboo at her back was impenetrable. To her front was an inferno.

There was no escape.

If only she could Send to Bryce, or any of her brothers and sisters.

Whispering a last goodbye, she waited for the fire to take her.

22

The heat was gone. No flames crackled. She could breathe again and the air was blissfully cool.

Her canister was wrenched from her hand. It hit the ground with a thump.

"Shall I restrain her, Lord?"

Lord?

Her eyes hadn't been playing tricks on her at the shuttle landing site. Only *he* would award himself such a ridiculous, highfalutin title.

"No need. Look at the state of her, and without elixir, she's useless." She felt a shadow block out the sunlight and the voice hissed in her ear, "You *are* useless, aren't you, Carina? Not so clever without your little stage prop. Bringing the Great Mage to her knees is pathetically easy."

Forcing her eyes open a slit, she beheld the man she'd seen in the vehicle giving orders. He'd Located them at the site despite Darius's Cloak. Clearly, it didn't shield from Casts. They'd never tested that capability.

Then after they'd Transported to the beach, he'd Located them again, and sent his soldiers in to capture or kill them. Transporting hundreds of meters away had made no difference at all. Another Cast and once more he'd found them. Finally, as soon as she'd stayed in one spot long enough, he'd managed to first Locate her and then Transport her to his side.

He was older than she remembered him. *Much* older. He'd aged so much he was barely recognizable, hence her shock and doubt. But it explained why the woman in the mountain caves resembled Ma, and why the entire planet seemed to be prepared for their arrival—set up to prevent her from achieving her goal of a peaceful life for her family.

"Castiel." Her voice was a mere croak.

"You do recognize me, then." He smirked. "I was wondering how long it would take until the penny dropped, or if I would have the pleasure of informing you myself."

He had to be in late middle age, if not older. His thick black hair had thinned to gray strands. The youthful visage of a mid-teens boy had creased into lines and wrinkles. Eyes that had once been round and deep brown were hooded and filmy.

How long had he traveled the galaxy? And how had he found Earth's coordinates? She'd taken the mage documents from the castle on Ostillon. He'd never even set eyes on them.

"Your little burnt face is alive with questions," he teased.

"I do have questions," she murmured, "but I'm not sure if you'll answer them."

His expression brightened with pleasure. He was enjoying himself. He must have anticipated this moment for decades, brooding over the revenge he would exact on his siblings for a childhood spent feeling inferior. His spitefulness made him weak. It was a weakness she could exploit—a weakness she had to exploit. Though her view of her surrounds was limited, Parthenia and Darius didn't seem to be here. She had to prevent him from doing the same to them as he had to her. She had to go through with her plan, albeit somewhat modified.

"Try me," he gloated. "Oh, and don't think I don't know what you're doing. You want to distract me so Parthenia and Darius have time to get away. Perhaps they might, but, one way or another, it doesn't matter. I can always Locate them again." He held up a fist. Parthenia's brooch and one of Darius's combs peeked from between his fingers. "What's more, I have you too, and they'll do anything to save you, as will Ferne and Oriana. Such are the bonds of familial love, as my dear Father knew so well. All I have to do is threaten to hurt you and they'll come running, falling over themselves in their efforts to protect you. I will enjoy destroying all of you, one by one, including Nahla and your oafish boyfriend. How odd you're still with him. But as they say, love is blind."

He leaned so close his face took up all her vision. "I can read your mind. I know what question burns at its center right now. You want to know how I arrived here ahead of you." He grinned. "For so many years I've anticipated informing you about what happened after you dumped me on Ostillon."

"When you betrayed us to Sable Dirksen, you mean?" Her voice sounded stronger. The effects of the fire were easing. She could breathe better and she didn't feel so weak, though her seared skin stung painfully.

"Betrayed is such a strong word. I prefer to see my actions as sensible and rational. Had I remained with Sable I would have eventually gained control of the Dirksen clan, vanquished the Sherrerrs once and for all, and taken my rightful place as supreme leader in the sector."

"Sable would have chewed you up and spat you out. Anyway, aren't you a bit old for all this? Clinging to the past isn't healthy."

"I believe *you* were the one who wanted to know what happened back then?"

She didn't answer, playing for time.

After a pause he seemed to conclude he'd scored a point. "You ruined my chances of success with the Dirksens, and the Sherrerrs only ever saw me as their slave. The sector was dead to me."

She had a strong feeling Castiel had ruined his own chances with the Dirksens, assuming he'd ever had any, but she remained quiet. He was on a roll.

"I decided to pay you back in kind. Why should you achieve your dream when I cannot? However, I didn't anticipate arriving before you. What kept you?" Before she could reply, he added, "It was a rhetorical question. You remember Justin? Jace's brother?"

She blinked. How had Castiel known about the mage brothers? She and the Black Dogs had taken Jace from his cell in the mountain castle, where Sable Dirksen had left him to starve, and the last time she'd seen Justin, a member of the Mage Council, had been on Pirine. She didn't know what had happened to him after the Dirksens had burned the Matching campsite. She'd assumed he'd escaped along with most of the other mages.

"You *do* remember him. I can tell."

Her heart quailed at what she imagined she was about to hear. "If you hurt him..."

"You'll do what? This may come as a surprise, but you aren't in a position to make threats. You see, I *did* hurt him. Rather a lot. But that was after he gave away his secrets to Kee. The commander is a master interrogator. I don't mind admitting it. We became reasonably good friends on our long voyage. I can see you're becoming confused, so I'll start at the beginning."

It was not confusion but compassion that was troubling her. Compassion for the kind, wise man who had suffered at her evil half-brother's hands, and regret that he'd been dragged into her business and suffered for it.

"After you abandoned me and set off on your Great Adventure..." he made air quotes with his fingers "...Kee returned to Ostillon. He knew from the Dirksens that I remained on the planet, and he sought me out to find a way he might rescue Sable. Only a mage knows what another mage can do. The poor man was deeply in love with her and prepared to stop at nothing to get her back safe and sound. But when word arrived from one of the mercenaries who resigned from your band that Sable was dead, his plan changed. He wanted nothing more than to make her executioner pay for the misdeed. He would do whatever it took to achieve his aim, and, believe me, when Kee wants something, he gets it. You and the rest of the mages might have departed Ostillon, but several had been captured on Pirine, Justin among them. I won't bore you with the details, but Kee wanted to help me follow you to Earth. Our desires dovetailed nicely. All we had to do was to wait for you to arrive, and here we are."

"The woman at the ancient mages' hideaway in the mountains—she's your daughter?"

He grimaced. "Letitia bears an unfortunate resemblance to our dear departed mother. I'm not surprised you understood who she must be."

"Letitia? What a pretty name. You must love her very much." She was being sarcastic. Castiel was incapable of loving anyone except himself.

His grimace deepened. "She's...useful. She's a mage, as you must have noticed, and not a bad one. Due to Mother's neglect of my education I couldn't teach her myself, but the mages here have done a reasonable job."

So there were more mages on Earth, and Castiel was in contact with them. Was he also controlling them? Did they know he was a Dark Mage? There was so much more she was dying to find out, but she had to act soon. He might grow bored of delighting in her downfall, and then he would seek out Parthenia and Darius. They could have already left on the shuttle but she doubted it. They were, as Castiel had said, loyal to a fault. She had to think of something to distract him, put him off his guard. What better distraction was there to a narcissist than to get him to talk about himself?

"You're an old man. Isn't devoting your entire life to getting back at me a little... excessive? You must have better things to do."

"Don't flatter yourself," he spat. "I've done plenty during my sojourn on Earth. Plenty. Dealing with you and the sad wastes-of-space who are our siblings is merely a pastime. I will take great pleasure in introducing you to my empire before deciding whether to—"

She'd fastened her hand around his throat. The simple movement sent waves of agony down her arm, but she squeezed hard, sealing off his voice and breathing. Castiel flailed, attracting the attention of his men, but before they could reach her she threw him on his back. Snatching the flask at his side, she ducked the rifle butt aimed at her head. And, as she'd hoped, no one wanted to risk a shot while she was so close to their 'Lord'.

Tearing the lid from the flask, she swigged elixir. Hands grabbed her shoulders, wrenching her to her feet, but at the same time she pulled Castiel's weapon from its holster and aimed it at him. "Release me or he's dead."

The hands left her. She quickly scooped up the items Castiel had been holding, which had fallen from his grasp. In her hand were Parthenia's brooch, Darius's comb, and a button that must have been torn from her jacket during the struggle with the guard. She then stared at her half-brother, sprawled on the ground. She had a short window of time while the elixir would retain its effect. "What's it to be, Castiel? Transport or Split?"

The arrogant confidence in his eyes wavered. "You won't do it. You wouldn't dare. Your own death would follow mine in an instant." But terror underlay his words. They'd both witnessed his father's horrible demise at Ma's hands.

"The satisfaction of knowing I'd removed you from the universe might be worth it." She closed her eyes.

"You don't have the guts to kill me, Carina Lin. Run back to our brothers and sisters if you like. I'm enjoying our game of cat and mouse, and I'll also enjoy bringing it to its inevitable conclusion."

23

Bryce was seriously pissed off. He hadn't spoken a word to Carina the entire shuttle ride back to the ship, and he'd maintained his silence in the hours afterward as she and her siblings came to grips with the fact that Castiel had re-entered their lives.

Bryce was the type of person to stew a while before voicing his grievance, so she left him to it. Nothing she could say would make a difference to how he felt anyway. He was right to be angry. If the roles were reversed she would have been angry too. Yet what she'd done was also right. She hadn't had a choice about it.

He waited until they were alone in their cabin before saying, "We need to talk."

She heaved a sigh. "I know." Sitting next to him on their bed, she took his hand. "I know what you're going to say, but—"

He removed his hand from her grasp. "You can't do that to me again. Ever. If you do, I don't think our relationship can stand it."

She took a breath. She knew he was upset, but not this upset. "Bryce, there was no time to explain or discuss it. I had to get you to safety, and I had to find Castiel. If I hadn't we would have forever been at risk of him Locating and Transporting Parthenia, Darius and me.

The only reason he didn't do it immediately was because we kept moving. He couldn't get a lock on us. As soon as he could, when you and I were hiding in the bamboo, he captured me. And I couldn't take you with me because..." Her words petered out.

Bryce's lips had thinned to a line and he'd turned pale. The anger he was holding back dismayed her.

"Because...?"

"Because it would have complicated things. If both of us had gone to Castiel he would have used you to force me to do whatever he wanted. He would have threatened to kill you, and then what else could I do except obey? You know what it was like with his father. Castiel learned all of Stefan Sherrerr's tricks."

"So you're saying I'm a liability? That I couldn't have helped you? That I'm incapable?"

"No!" She covered her face with her hands. "You don't understand."

"I think I do. You wanted to play the hero, again."

"That isn't true! And it's not fair. Do you really think I'm so crazy I would risk burning to death just to inflate my ego? You saw how I was before Parthenia Healed me. Do you think I nearly died for fun?" She hadn't told him or anyone else that she *would* have died if Castiel hadn't Transported her. No one knew she'd spilled the remains of her elixir. It had seemed an unnecessary detail. Now she didn't think she would ever reveal the truth. Not if this was Bryce's reaction without that tidbit.

"No, not for fun." His tone was softer. "But the first thing you thought was you had to get me out of the way before tackling the problem yourself. Because you're the only one who could do it."

"That's ridiculous. I'm sorry you're hurt, but let's not pussyfoot around the facts. I was the only one who could do it. Out of the two of us, who can Cast, huh?" Perhaps her abilities did emasculate him but she couldn't help it. She couldn't deny who she was.

"Wow, that's some apology. Thanks. I feel much better."

"I'm not trying to make you feel better, I'm trying to make you see sense. There wasn't anything else I could do in the circumstances except exactly what I did. If I hadn't Transported you to the shuttle and gone after Castiel we would probably all be dead right now, Bibik included. Castiel would have Located Darius and Parthenia in the shuttle and discovered where it was. We were lucky he didn't spot us when we first landed. I guess he wasn't Casting for us then. He can't do it all the time or it would exhaust him. We would be dead or captured, and then he would have enticed Ferne and Oriana to the surface—"

"For fuck's sake, Carina. I get it!" Bryce rose to his feet and leaned over her, fists clenched. "Do you think I can live with your family for years and not understand how it works? I was there when Stefan Sherrerr kidnapped you. I was there when you escaped the *Nightfall*. I've been there, right by your side, all the time. I left my family to help yours. I gave up my future on Ithiya. I've risked my life again and again to help you. Have you forgotten all that? Or do you only see me as a pathetic hanger-on, tagging along because I don't have anything better to do? Or perhaps I'm just a lovesick nobody with no life of their own?"

She looked up at him, tears pooling in her eyes. She swallowed. "No, I don't think any of that. I love y—"

"Do you? Do you really? Is that what love is? Ignoring my wishes? Riding roughshod over my free will? Transporting me wherever you want whenever you feel like it? What else have you done? Have you Enthralled me like you did Parthenia? Did you do a little interrogation late at night while I was too sleepy to notice? Or maybe you got me to agree to something against my will. That's a funny kind of love."

"I've never Enthralled you," she whispered.

"How would I know? How can I trust you when you just Transport me out of a situation without a by-your-leave?"

"There wasn't time for anything else! How can you expect me to ignore the dangers and not do what's needed to save your life, just so you don't feel controlled?" She reached out and touched his arm. He didn't pull it away, to her great relief. "I can guess how it must feel, and, if anything, I would be even angrier. Of the two of us, I *am* the one with the bigger ego, I admit."

He didn't react, ignoring her attempt to make eye contact.

"I don't know what I'm supposed to do," she continued. "We're different. I can do things you can't, and if I and my siblings couldn't Cast we wouldn't have made it this far."

"If you and your family couldn't Cast we wouldn't even be here."

It was an undeniable truth. The blessing and curse of their abilities was what had prompted her to drag everyone halfway across the galaxy.

"The only reason we met was because I'm a mage," she said quietly. "I was on Ithiya to find Darius and try to make contact with a mage family."

Bryce sat down beside her, his shoulders high and head low as he rested his elbows on his knees. "I guess that's right," he murmured. "If you weren't who you are we wouldn't be together."

A scene from a few days ago returned to her mind, when they'd been in the Twilight Dome and she'd asked him if he had any regrets. He'd said he hadn't. Was that still true? She didn't dare ask him. Perhaps he was concluding he'd made a mistake.

"I don't know how to make things better," she said. "I don't know if I can promise to never Cast on you again without your permission in a life-and-death situation. I love you. I don't want you to die." The practical part of her mind protested. *Of course* she should save him if it came down to it. She would want him to save her. Yet she empathized with his reaction to what she'd done. For once, she managed to not speak the quiet part out loud.

He took her hand in his, but his focus remained downward. Gently, he rubbed it. "I don't know how to make things better either. Maybe we can't."

She stiffened, dreading what might follow.

"It's funny," he said. "I love that you're a mage. I love that about you, though I think I would love you just the same if you weren't. But it means we aren't equals, and nothing can change that. Maybe that's something I've been trying to ignore for too long." He released her hand and stood up, continuing to not meet her gaze. "I need time to think. I'm going to sleep elsewhere for a while."

"No, don't," she protested, a catch in her voice. "Let's talk some more. We can find a way through this."

"You're not hearing me—again."

She was silent.

Before he left, he said, "What happened today... That's why ordinary people hate mages. You make us feel useless. If you want to live safely on Earth, you'll have to figure out a way to fix that problem."

24

After hours of tossing and turning Carina was finally falling asleep when she felt the ship move. It wasn't easy to feel the motion of a behemoth like the *Bathsheba*, but she'd spent so long aboard her she'd become sensitive to any deviation from the norm.

She comm'd the bridge, but received no answer.

She tried Hsiao instead. The pilot probably had a good reason for changing their position, but it would have been nice to be consulted.

Hsiao also ignored her comm.

As the movement continued, Carina grew alarmed. Was someone else moving the ship? In her sleepy state, she wondered if enemies boarded and everyone except her been taken prisoner. It was a wild thought, but no other explanation sprang immediately to mind. She couldn't check if Bryce knew what was happening, not after their argument and his request for her to leave him alone. She comm'd Parthenia.

To her relief, her sister answered quickly. "What's wrong? I was sound asleep."

"You're okay?"

"Of course I'm okay."

"Is Bibik with you?"

"Yes. Why?"

"Have you noticed the ship's moving?"

"No, she... Oh, you're right. She is. That's odd."

Carina cut the comm. If Bibik wasn't flying the *Bathsheba* it had to be Hsiao, or perhaps a trainee pilot. Maybe that was the explanation. But it was risky to practice maneuvers in the current situation. One thing she knew for sure—she wasn't going to get to sleep until she knew what was going on.

She got out of bed, pulled on a robe, and walked to the bridge.

Hsiao, who sat at the pilot's station, ducked her head as she walked in.

Van Hasty was here and so was Jackson, Rees, Mads, Berkcan, Ola, and Pamuk. Even Chi-tang was present. He'd managed to give Cheepy the slip.

"Well," Carina said, "isn't this quite the delegation? Is anyone going to tell me what's going on?"

Everyone looked at Van Hasty, except Hsiao, who kept her gaze steadfastly ahead.

"We decided to take matters into our own hands," Van Hasty said, a defiant look in her eye.

We?

Carina had a strong suspicion the merc had persuaded the others to gang together and back her up.

"And that means...?"

Had the Black Dogs decided to give up the idea of settling on Earth and return across the galaxy?

Jackson cleared his throat. "We're going to take out that place your asshole little brother is running. One blast from the Obliterator should do it—and take him out at the same time. Then your problems will be over and we can go planetside."

That explained Chi-tang's presence. He was the weapon's operator.

"Are you all insane?" Carina spluttered. "Hsiao, stop the ship."

Hsiao looked at Van Hasty, who shook her head.

"Hsiao," Carina repeated, "do what I said. That's a direct order."

"You're long past the stage of giving us orders, Lin," said Van Hasty.

"You might have made corporal in the Black Dogs but you were discharged a long time ago, and we're not even running your contract anymore. When was the last time you paid us?"

"But you know why we're here. You agreed to help my family. You said I still had six days."

"Five days. But it doesn't matter, not now we figured out a faster way to do it."

"Your way isn't faster or better. It's stupid. If you blow up that site it'll ruin everything, not to mention the fact that you'll be killing hundreds if not thousands of innocent people."

"Innocent?" Jackson's forehead creased into a quizzical frown. "You think those men and women working for your brother can't tell what an evil, traitorous shithole he is? But they're still working for him. Choose the wrong side and you get what's coming to you. That's what I say."

His merc companions nodded their agreement.

"Okay," Carina reasoned, "if you don't care about murdering Castiel's workers, think about the damage you'll be doing to our prospects on Earth. By all accounts it's a peaceful place, as close to a harmonious human society as you can get. How do you think unleashing the Obliterator is going to go down? What kind of introduction is that? How will the people of Earth see us?"

A puzzled look passed between the mercs.

"Why should we care?" Van Hasty asked.

"Because we want a new life, a different life, an end to all the violence and killing."

"We do?"

"First I heard about it," said Pamuk.

"Yeah," Jackson growled, "I think you're getting confused, Lin. No one here signed up to the happy-ever-after scenario you have in mind. I can't speak for everyone, but what I'm looking forward to is getting wasted and seeing some different ugly mugs for a change."

"*You're* wanted for murder," Carina said, "in case you forgot."

Jackson was another problem to be overcome. While Earth might be peaceful—on the surface—it was also technologically advanced.

Jackson was known to the authorities. He wouldn't last five minutes in even a small town before being picked up.

"Are you a little old to be getting wasted?" she added. "Don't you want to settle down?"

Another look passed between the Dogs. This time it was incredulity.

Jackson gave a great bark of laughter and doubled over, clutching his sides. His companions seemed to find her comment equally funny. The atmosphere in the bridge reverberated with their whoops and giggles until finally Jackson pulled himself together sufficiently to squeeze out, "Good one, Lin."

The *Bathsheba* had to be nearly out of the Moon's cover. Soon, she would be visible to anyone on Earth who happened to have a telescope pointing in the right direction. Perhaps it wasn't important. Perhaps whoever had covered up the movements of the spy space vessel would do the same for the colony ship, but she didn't want to take the risk.

"Hsiao, please stop the ship."

The pilot shrugged helplessly. "It's seven against one. Sorry."

"Chi-tang?" Carina appealed to the pickup from Lakshmi Station. "You could refuse to fire. Then we might as well stay behind the Moon."

"Someone else could do it, and, besides, Van Hasty's promised she'll get Cheepy off my back."

"You would kill hundreds of people just to get rid of a nagging ex-girlfriend?"

"Like I said, if I don't do it someone else will. And she's *really* annoying."

The mercs nodded vigorously.

Carina opened a comm. "Darius?"

He was still awake, probably playing games on his interface. "Hi, Carina. You're up late."

"Could you Cloak the ship? I'll explain why later."

"Uhh, sure."

"A waste of time," Van Hasty commented as Carina closed the comm. "They'll know our position as soon as we fire."

"We're *not* firing," she said between her teeth.

How could she make them see sense? It wasn't only her family's happiness at stake. The hilarity the mercs had expressed at the idea of living out the rest of their lives as ordinary, law-abiding citizens wasn't shared by them all. It wasn't hard to keep track of general opinion in the closed confines of a starship, and her impression was that most of the passengers were hoping to integrate into Earth society and finally begin living normal lives. The bunch of Dogs on the bridge were the die-hards, holding onto their military mindsets.

Were their old habits also responsible for their decision to wreak havoc on Earth? Maybe it was only that, after the long, monotonous voyage, they were simply itching for a fight.

The ship had to be entirely out from the Moon's cover, and Darius's Cloak wouldn't last forever.

"You can't do this!" she exclaimed. "We came here to start a new life, a better life."

Van Hasty shook her head. "You were always a dreamer, Lin. But things don't change. People don't change. Humans have always killed each other and they always will. That's why we have to swing first. It might not seem like it but we're doing you a favor. If we wait around and play nice, your brother's gonna be here soon enough to wipe us out."

"Should I start the power up sequence?" Chi-tang asked.

"Yeah, do it."

Carina tried to think of a way to stop them, but she was out of arguments. And Hsiao was right: it was seven against one. She couldn't force them to stop. Her fingers bit into her palms as the *Bathsheba* slowly built up speed on her journey to Earth orbit. "*Please.* Don't do this."

Jackson patted her on the shoulder. "In a day or so you'll be thanking us."

The bridge door slid open. Bryce had arrived. He walked in, rubbing his eyes. "What's going on? Where are we going, and why's the bridge comm dead?" He didn't seem surprised to see her but neither did he acknowledge her presence.

Van Hasty quickly outlined the plan.

"But isn't that gonna screw everything up?"

"That's what I've been trying to tell them," Carina said.

"Don't worry," said Jackson. "We've got everything in hand."

Bryce frowned. "No, no, no. That isn't going to work. Carina's got the right idea. You have to play this carefully. Earth's different from other planets. You can't go in there guns blazing. Not if you want to live there long term."

"Yeah, about that," Jackson replied. "I can't say I've spent a lot of time down there, but from what I could tell and what I've heard, Earth seems pretty boring. It won't hurt to shake things up a little."

"But that isn't what Carina wants."

Pamuk puffed a derisive *Pfft*. "Who gives a shit?" adding, "Sorry, but you know what I mean."

Carina wasn't sure she did know, but she was grateful for Bryce's arrival.

"I do," he said, "and so does her family, and more than half this ship, I bet, including the Marchonish women. They want to follow her lead and take things slow and easy. That's why you cut the bridge comm, right? So you could act unilaterally. Then, when the deed's done, everyone has to join the battle. Better to ask forgiveness than permission, yeah?"

The less outspoken mercs began to look uncomfortable. Jackson's expression was pensive, but Van Hasty remained defiant. "Who the hell are you to lecture us? You're not even a Black Dog."

"Maybe not, but Carina was, and she deserves your loyalty. I thought that's what the Dogs were about. I thought you guys supported each other. Even if you don't think she's going about this the right way, you should give her a chance."

"She's had a chance, and we don't owe her anything."

"Yes, you do. You all owe her your lives."

"If you're talking about all the shit that's gone down after Cadwallader accepted her miserable assignment—"

"I'm not. I'm talking about before then." He turned to Carina. "You never told them, did you?"

"Umm." She actually didn't know what he was referring to but she didn't want to let on, not now he seemed to be getting through to the mercs. "No, I never did."

"It was just before the mission to rescue Darius from the Dirksens," Bryce continued to them. "You were supposed to be protecting an embassy, only your old boss had signed you up to a bum deal. The enemy had far greater numbers and you were going to be massacred."

Now she remembered, though she didn't recall telling Bryce about it. The event must have come up in one of their many conversations about their pasts. It had been the first time she'd been forced to make a Cast while on duty that couldn't be easily explained away.

Jackson's eyes widened and he stared at her. "That was *you*!"

During the embassy siege, when it had become clear all the mercs were about to die if she didn't do something drastic, she had Transported the enemy soldiers a fair distance away, giving the Dogs time to escape.

"You mean when..." Van Hasty's shoulders slumped. "... I was pinned down, no way out. Toast. Then the hostiles were gone. Vanished. I couldn't believe it. All these years, and I never put two and two together. How dumb is that? Did Cadwallader know?"

"He figured it out," Carina replied. "Later, after I'd hired the Dogs to help me on Ostillon and I had to explain to him what I can do. Captain Speidel knew, though. I had to tell him I was a mage to explain how I knew Darius's location."

"I remember Speidel," said Rees. "Good guy."

"I was there at the embassy," Pamuk said. "Got wounded. A medic told me I nearly bled out. *Damn.*"

Silence filled the room.

After a few moments, Hsiao said, "Shall I, er, return the ship to her previous position?"

"Yeah," Van Hasty answered grudgingly.

The mercs began to file out. Chi-tang got up from his seat and trotted up to Van Hasty. "We still have a deal, right?"

Carina thanked Bryce. He didn't answer, only gave her a pained look as he left.

Chi-tang still at her heels, Van Hasty was the last to depart the bridge. Before the door closed behind her, she said, "Five days."

25

Officer Matt was missing. Apparently, no one had given him an ear comm and his cabin assignment didn't appear on the manifest. In a ship as vast as the *Bathsheba* it was going to be hard to track him down. Carina had tried the places she might expect to find him—the Twilight Dome, all the refectories, gyms, and various entertainment centers—but he wasn't in any of them. Asking around, she discovered that in his short time on the ship he'd become well known and well liked, though she got the impression most of the passengers thought he was a little crazy. That was probably due to his belief that everything around him was part of a gigantic hoax. But no one had seen him since the previous active shift.

She cast her mind back to the last time she'd seen the man from Earth. It had been at the debriefing Van Hasty and Jackson had crashed...along with Ava. Ava had taken Matt with her when she left, telling him she would find him a cabin.

Carina comm'd the Marchonish woman, but she didn't answer.

Why does everything have to be so hard?

She checked with the sick bay staff. Ava's shift didn't start for several hours.

Cursing, she set off for the woman's abode.

The Marchonish women had taken over a small section of the living quarters. Understandably, after their experiences at the hands of their planet's menfolk, they'd been nervous around the mercs, who were mostly male, burly, and loud. The men had also avoided the women, not knowing how to treat them. They were used to female mercs, who were clear, and often physical, in their rebukes if a guy tried to take things further than they wanted. Over time some of the men had learned how to be quieter and gentler and to listen a bit better, and relationships between Black Dogs and the newcomers had formed.

The Marchonish women's section had begun to empty somewhat as couples moved into double cabins in other areas, but several of the women remained, including Ava. Carina guessed her friends helped her out with childcare while she worked.

She rang the door chime.

After waiting a minute, she rang the chime again.

Perhaps Ava was deeply asleep and her comm's alert hadn't woken her. Carina felt a bit bad waking her up, but this matter couldn't wait.

The door slid open, but only part of the way. Ava was tousle-haired, flushed, and wearing a bath robe. "Hi, Carina. I didn't expect to see you here."

"Sorry to wake you. I'm looking for Matt. Do you remember which cabin he was assigned?"

"Oh." Ava's flush deepened. "Why do you want him? Is it urgent?"

"Yes, very."

"Uhh, well..." She looked over her shoulder and then back at Carina, her face deep red.

A male voice within the room murmured something.

Shit.

Carina internally groaned. "I'm really sorry to disturb you. I'll give you a minute."

"Thanks." The door closed.

Leaning her back against the bulkhead, she rolled her eyes.

She's only known him a few days!

When those Marchonish women set their sights on someone, they moved *fast*.

Matt appeared, buttoning his shirt. He looked mildly abashed but not to Ava's level. "You want me for something?"

"I do, but..." She peeked in the cabin. Ava was tidying her bedding. She called out to her. "Could I speak to you too?"

After another minute, she came out, dressed.

"Sorry about this," Carina said awkwardly. "But I'm glad you seem to be settling in, Matt."

"Thanks. I like Ava, but nothing's changed. You're holding an officer of the law against his will, which is a serious crime. You'll pay for it when everything comes to light, though I guess you could plead insanity."

She turned to Ava. "He still believes this isn't real?"

"I've tried to explain but nothing I say seems to convince him."

He placed a hand on her arm. "I believe that *you* believe it. That's all that matters. I don't think you're deliberately lying."

Ava looked at Carina appealingly.

But she didn't know how to convince him either. When a place was so technologically advanced anything could be faked, it became impossible to tell reality from fiction.

She took them to a small, out-of-the-way room with a machine that dispensed beverages. As she'd hoped, it was empty. When everyone was settled, she began. "Matt, I need information about Earth, information we can't get through regular channels. Something strange is going on down there and I have to find out what exactly is happening. If I can't, it's going to make everything much harder for my family and maybe everyone else on this ship, Ava included. Things could be very dangerous for us if we try to settle on the planet."

He smiled indulgently. "Whatever you want to ask me, go ahead. But I warn you, I'm just an ordinary guy. I don't have access to classified information."

He was humoring her, but there was no reason he had to believe the *Bathsheba* was a real starship or that her passengers were from other planets in order to answer her questions.

"Setting your conclusion that this is all a hoax aside, *hypothetically*, if people had arrived from outer space decades ago and infiltrated Earth's governments, how would someone go about addressing it? Who would they approach?"

His eyebrows lifted. "This is worse than I thought. You seriously think all the governments are corrupt?"

"Not necessarily corrupt, but compromised. You see, mages have the ability to influence others' behavior and decisions. A mage could persuade key people to erase data, ignore information, replace files with false ones, and they wouldn't even remember doing it. An evil mage, working with others, could exert a lot of control over Earth's population."

"That's a pretty powerful spell you have there," Matt replied, chuckling.

Carina's jaw muscle twitched. "It's not a..."

Ava shrugged.

Carina took a breath and started again. "I know you don't believe me, but can you put your doubts aside just for a second and think hard? I need your help. Earth needs your help. Imagine what I'm saying might be true. As a police officer you have a duty to protect people and to bring lawbreakers to justice, don't you?"

He'd been taking a sip of his drink. He put the mug down before replying, "*If* what you're saying were true, I still couldn't help you. These 'mages' as you call them could be anywhere and everywhere, casting spells left, right, and center, tricking government officials into thinking black is white. If that was really happening, how could anyone stop them? As soon as they tried, or they were caught snooping or whatever, the mage would only have to get into their head and change what they thought. Or..." he waggled his fingers "... make them disappear in a puff of smoke."

"We can't change what others think. Not in the long term."

"Then disappearing people seems more likely. Whatever. It's moot. You're insane, and the sooner you let me go the better." He turned to Ava. "I'll make sure nothing bad happens to you. You're a victim here."

"I really do come from a distant star system, you know."

"Of course you do." He put an arm around her and kissed her cheek. Then he said to Carina, "Is there anything else you wanted to speak to me about?"

"No. You can go."

Matt and Ava left, holding hands.

26

The five days Van Hasty had reminded Carina of had shrunk to four with no sign of a solution to her problems.

Parthenia came to see her. "What's wrong with Bryce?" she asked as she stepped into the cabin.

That was the great thing about siblings: they didn't bother with social niceties.

"Hi," Carina replied. "I'm doing fine. How are you?"

"There's no need to be snippy. He's been walking around with his sad puppy look for two days. Have you two been fighting?" She glanced around the room. "Is he even sleeping here?"

"He's taking some time away from me to think."

"Ugh." Parthenia sank onto the sofa. "That bad, huh? What did you fight about?"

"It isn't important. Mage and non-mage relationships are hard."

"I'm not sure that's true. Bibik and I get along okay, and so do Ferne and his endless stream of girlfriends."

"Don't exaggerate. He's only on his third."

"Which isn't bad going, considering the limited pool of candidates. Anyway, he always breaks up with them amicably. Maybe it's because he grew up so close to Oriana."

"So it's me who's the difficult one. Thanks. That makes me feel a whole lot better."

"I'm just saying..." Parthenia took another look around the cabin. "It will be nice to leave this place, don't you think? I mean, in many ways the *Bathsheba* is our home, but I would love to live in a house and be able to step outside to feel the sun on my skin."

"Me too," Carina replied glumly. "At the moment I can't see how that's going to happen. Castiel has made Earth out of bounds, and he's fixed things so the entire population is on the lookout for us. Even if we hid ourselves away somewhere remote, I'm sure he would find us in the end. And if Castiel didn't, Commander Kee would. That man's a machine. How was I to know when I executed Sable Dirksen I was killing the love of his life?"

"Hmm. You didn't tell us about Kee. I didn't know he was here too. He was the man who attempted to massacre the mages at the Matching on Pirine, right?"

"That's him, though he would have been working under Sable's orders. I must have forgotten to tell you Castiel mentioned him. Our lovely brother had a lot to say. I had a feeling he'd been rehearsing his speech for years."

"You also didn't tell us that it was Castiel, not you, who got you out of that fire."

"No, it wasn't."

Parthenia gave her a hard look.

"All right. It was Castiel who Transported me. I'd spilled my elixir."

"I knew your story didn't make any sense. How could you have found him so easily? No one's that lucky. So if Castiel hadn't accidentally saved you, you would have died. Is that what's upsetting Bryce?"

"No, he doesn't know. Don't tell him, Parthenia."

She held up her hands. "I'm certainly not going to interfere in your business. I'm only concerned about impediments to our settling on Earth. I understand now that not only Castiel stands in our way. We also have to contend with this man, Kee."

"I don't know which is worse. Our brother is evil to the core, but Kee is damned smart."

"A formidable pair. But Earth is vast. Surely we should be able to find somewhere to live. As long as we're careful—"

"As long as we skulk around, keep to the shadows, pretend we don't have our abilities. We didn't come all this way to live the same life we lived where we grew up—a half-life, always watching, always fearing discovery."

"No, we didn't. But sometimes it's better to bend than break. If we can't live openly we can still live, still take some pleasure in life. I'm tired of eating printed food, Carina. I'm sick of looking out at black, lonely space. All my adult years have been spent aboard a starship. I need something new. I need to *live*." She swallowed and added, "Even if it means never Casting again."

"You would give up who you are?"

"Being a mage isn't all I am," Parthenia whispered and looked down. Tears dropped onto her hands, lying on her lap.

Carina's sister had learned from a young age to suppress her true emotions. If she had worn her heart on her sleeve, her father would have known how much she hated him and loved her mother, drawing his wrath down on both of them. Covering up how she felt had become somewhat of a habit. For her to be in this state meant she was near the end of her tether.

Carina moved next to Parthenia and hugged her. "I'll find a way. Don't worry."

"There has to be some kind of way, a compromise of some kind."

"Maybe you're right. Maybe I've been going about this wrong, butting heads and acting before thinking." She recalled the Black Dogs on the bridge and smiled wryly. "Perhaps I'm more merc than mage."

The door chime sounded.

"My, I'm popular today."

Darius had come to see her too, with Nahla. Parthenia quickly wiped away her tears as they walked in.

"Are we having a family reunion?" Nahla quipped brightly.

"It looks like it," Carina replied. "I expect Ferne and Oriana will be along any minute. Is this purely a social call or do you want to see me about something in particular?"

Nahla sat next to Parthenia. "Isn't it obvious why we're here? We want to know when is the next trip to Earth. I would like to go this time. I'm the only one who hasn't been there yet. I've been reading all about it but I haven't had a chance to set eyes on the place."

Of all her siblings, Nahla was the one Carina was most reluctant to take to Earth. Though she was bright as a button, she didn't have mage or military skills. The revelation that Castiel was there only increased Carina's reluctance. Castiel bore a special hatred for his youngest sister, possibly even greater than the hatred he harbored toward Carina. Nahla had once been his biggest fan, but she'd switched sides—an act he would never forgive.

"I don't want to return to Earth without a plan," said Carina, "and I'm all out of ideas. As Officer Matt pointed out to me a few hours ago, Castiel seems to have everyone with any influence on Earth under his control. He's discovered and enlisted the mages there to his cause. They're all working for him. What good are our abilities now? What can we do against hundreds, potentially thousands, of mages?"

"He's enlisted them to his cause?" Nahla asked. "That doesn't sound like Castiel. He was never the persuasive type. He would have thought it beneath him."

Carina frowned. "I'd just assumed..."

"Believe me, I know our nasty brother better than anyone. I would be very surprised if Castiel has used diplomacy to recruit a workforce. That isn't his style."

"You're right. He must be controlling them somehow."

"If we could find out what he's doing," Darius said, "maybe we could put a stop to it. Then Earth would be a friendlier place to us."

"It would be a huge task, though," said Carina, "and we wouldn't know where to start. We have no contacts. We don't know anyone down there who can help us discover how Castiel is exerting his control. If we reveal that we're from outsystem, we'll..." She frowned again.

"We'll what?" Parthenia asked. "Are you thinking about the General Alert?"

"We *do* have friends down there," Carina blurted. "There *are* people who will believe us and who might help."

"Ha!" Nahla grinned. "You mean the Exodus Testifiers."

"They would be ecstatic if planetary colonists turned up on their doorstep. It would prove they weren't cranks. They would be vindicated."

"But wouldn't it put them in danger from Castiel?" asked Darius. "He could kill anyone who associates with us."

"Yes, we would have to be careful. We would have to let them know the stakes." Yet, somehow, she felt sure the Testifiers would agree to help them.

27

The journalist who had written the article about the Exodus Testifier was as unscrupulous as they came. It hadn't taken more than a little prompting and the promise of exclusive rights to a recording for him to give up the real name and the address of his interviewee. What proved a lot harder was reaching the man.

The address was many kilometers from the site where it had been safe to land the shuttle, and traveling by public transportation was out of the question. Not only was no one from the *Bathsheba* 'chipped', the surveillance systems would be primed to pick up Carina, Bryce, and Darius's faces due to their arrest on the first visit to Earth. Neither did they dare risk Transporting, so they had to walk to the Testifier's location.

He lived a great distance from Officer Matt's little town, in a city on another continent, yet the place resembled their initial experience of Earth. No motorized traffic traveled the roads, only mechanical conveyances, and many people simply walked. Delivery bots trundled the pathways, carrying their loads to their destinations, ignored by pedestrians. Metro stations were everywhere. The subsurface had to be a honeycomb of tunnels.

The ambient noise was minimal, only the chatter of voices, the clanks and clinks of bicycles and larger pedal-driven vehicles, and the faint hum of the bots. Trees and shrubs lined the streets. It seemed a plant grew in every available space, including the rooftops, which were a sea of long grasses. As they walked, Carina didn't spot anyone tending the vegetation. It appeared to have been planted—or perhaps grew naturally—to thrive in the local conditions.

Nahla had spent most of their journey vacillating between open-mouthed wonder and childlike excitement.

Bryce didn't speak to Carina as they walked, though not because he was punishing her. He wasn't like that. He was only melancholy. So was she. The end of their relationship seemed to be looming and she didn't know a way to save it. Their fundamental differences had overcome them. Perhaps it was always this way with mages and non-mages in the end.

"I like it here so much," said Oriana, trailing her hand over a flowering vine hanging from a house front. "It's so nice to be surrounded by green after living for years on a starship. And breathe the air! No faint sweatiness the filters can't scrub out."

Ferne halted. "This is it. Number 68."

Like most of the other houses they'd passed in this residential area of the Earth city, the Exodus Testifier's was two-story and had plants growing in pockets set into the front walls. The vegetation was unkempt, unlike many of the other homes. It was clear the householder wasn't interested in the upkeep of his vertical garden. In fact, the plants seemed to be weeds that had sprouted there opportunistically from blown-in seeds.

"Do you think he'll offer us a drink?" asked Oriana. "I'm so thirsty. Perhaps I could ask him for one. Do you think he'll mind?"

Carina exhaled, puffing out her lips. "Darius, are you getting anything? Anything we need to worry about?"

He was best at sensing evilness emanating from another mage, such as his horrible eldest brother and the Dark Mage, Wei, on Magog, but he also picked up on the internal life of non-mages. He closed his eyes and concentrated before replying, "I'm mostly getting Oriana, but very little from in there."

Oriana's eyes narrowed. "What do you mean, you're mostly getting me?"

Hoping Darius's impression was a good sign, Carina pressed the chime.

Grey-haired, mid-fifties and well into middle-aged spread the article had said, though the Testifier's name was not John Markham, but Alfie Binger. The door opened, revealing a man fitting the description. He was even wearing a cardigan and slacks.

"Sorry," Alfie said as his gaze quickly took in the six people on his doorstep, "I'm not interes—"

As he'd closed the door, Carina had shoved her foot in the gap. He looked down at the impediment preventing him from dismissing his unwelcome callers and then up at her face.

"We aren't selling anything," said Carina. "We want to talk to you about Exodus Testifiers."

His expression hardened. "In that case, I'm definitely not interested. Are you here because of the article? I did not give permission for that to be published. That man lied to me. Leave me alone. Move your foot or I'll call the police."

"We only want to talk to you for a few minutes. Let us in and we can explain."

"Absolutely not. Stop pestering me and go away."

"We're here because we want to be Testifiers too," Oriana said brightly. "We've seen the evidence and we believe it. Please let us in. We've walked so far, and I'm dreadfully thirsty."

"You want to join the Association?" Alfie asked suspiciously. "But you're foreigners." He pointed at their translators. "Join it in your own country."

"We live here," said Carina. "We aren't reporters. Think about it. Why would a media station send *six* people to talk to you?"

His gaze traveled from face to face and the tension seemed to go out of his body. "Okay, you can come in. But if I find out you're lying I'm calling the police and I'll press charges."

Alfie Binger's home was as cluttered as the article had implied. Boxes and stacks of printed material stood each side of his hall, the only available floor space dedicated to a path one-person wide. They followed him in single file to a lounge area, similarly filled with objects. There was more variety here. As well as more boxes and printed sheets, models of starships stood on every flat surface and hung from the ceiling. Pictures of starships and their crews in uniforms, smiling, festooned the walls. Piles of rations the article had mentioned filled the sitting areas.

"You're related, aren't you?" Alfie asked as he moved the ration packets onto the floor. "I can see the family resemblance." Straightening up, he added, looking at Bryce, "But not you. Are you the feisty one's boyfriend or something?"

Carina was tempted to reply *Something* but she kept her comment to herself. "What can you tell us about the Exodus? We don't know much, and we were hoping you could fill us in." It seemed a safer opening gambit than immediately revealing the real reason for their visit.

"Oh, before we start," said Oriana, "could I please have some water?"

Ferne tutted.

"Err." Alfie's suspicion appear to resurface. "All right. But you mustn't touch anything."

Bryce was navigating obstacles to move closer to the pictures on the walls.

"Oriana, could you stop thinking about your own comfort for once?" Ferne complained. "This is serious business."

"Carina," said Bryce, "look at this."

Oriana replied to Ferne, "How can I concentrate when my mouth is like your armpit?"

"You have no idea what my armpit's like," Ferne retorted.

"Oh shut up," said Nahla. "Both of you."

"*Carina*," Bryce repeated.

Alfie returned with a glass of water, which he handed to Oriana.

"Thank you so much." She gulped it down. "That's much better."

"Please sit," said Alfie. "Sit down, everyone."

They squeezed into the scant sitting space except for Bryce, who remained at the wall, hands in pockets as he scrutinized an image.

"What do you already know about the Exodus?" Alfie asked. "I'm just asking because there's no point in me repeating anything to you."

"Uhh, just the basics," Carina replied. "That people used to leave

Earth to colonize the stars. But we've forgotten about it, right? There isn't much evidence left. Do you know why?"

Alfie lifted his hands in a gesture of bewilderment. "Beats me. But the evidence is there for anyone who looks for it. I suppose the establishment doesn't like having its views challenged."

"Carina, look at this," Bryce insisted.

Alfie said, "You like that one, do you? She's one of my favorites too. Not the most beautiful example of her kind, but special nonetheless."

"Where did you get this picture?" asked Bryce.

"It's in the national archives. A perfect example of historians ignoring what's right under their noses. They say it's an artist's creation, a work of the imagination. All I can say is, if I was an artist I would draw something that looked a bit better. If you study the picture closely, it's perfectly obvious what everything's for."

While Alfie had been talking, Carina had worked her way across the crowded room to Bryce's side. He was looking at a 2D representation of a starship.

It took less than a second for recognition to dawn.

The drawing was simple, without schematics, as if the creator had only wanted to record the external appearance of the ship. The background was plain white, not a starscape as the real backdrop would have been. A ship this vast could only have been constructed in space.

Her pulse beating in her ears, Carina turned to Alfie. "This vessel —what do you know about her?"

"The ZSS *Hangxing Zhe*? She was the last colony ship ever built. I bet you didn't know that, huh? What a ship she must have been. The pinnacle of starship technology. And most of it lost now, of course. So much knowledge just…gone." He heaved a sigh.

The Hangxing Zhe. *So that's her real name.*

On the wall hung a picture of the *Bathsheba*.

28

Alfie Binger chuckled uneasily. His gaze flicked between each of them in turn, as if he was trying to probe the truth from their eyes. He got to his feet, stepped carefully through his hoard of Exodus paraphernalia to the window, and peered through the blinds. Then he walked to the other side of the room, where double glass doors gave a view of his overgrown yard. Craning his neck to right and left, he checked the rear of his house.

He turned to face them. "This is a joke, isn't it? A set up. Did that journalist send you here?" He scanned their bodies. "Is one of you recording this?" Though his words were aggressive his tone was semi-hopeful, as if he wanted to be proven wrong.

"No one is recording anything," Carina replied. "What I've told you is absolutely, one hundred percent true. It isn't a joke, or a lie."

They'd anticipated the Exodus Testifier might not believe they were from a starship, but no one had been able to think of a way to prove it. Any piece of technology small enough to carry could easily be from Earth. They couldn't expect him to be able to tell that it wasn't. As they'd discovered with Matt, when everything could be faked proving anything was hard. They would have to rely on Alfie taking them at their word, at least at first.

Carina hadn't told him the part about them being mages, sensing it could be a step too far and tip him over the edge into disbelief. If he kicked them out it would end any hope of having an Earth person on their side.

He took a deep breath and exhaled. "All right, let's say for now that I believe you, and that you really did arrive on the *Hangxing Zhe*, how could the ship have survived all this time? By Testifiers' reckoning she left at least two thousand years ago."

"Two thousand years in Earth time," Carina said. "You're forgetting the time dilation effect. While thousands of years passed here, the *Bathsheba*—I mean *Hangxing Zhe*—might only have been in existence for hundreds of years. We don't actually know how old she is. All we know is she's very old and she has technology that's unknown in the galactic sector I'm from."

She meant the self-repairing surfaces she'd discovered after the battle for the ship, but there was more about the *Bathsheba* that she'd never seen before. She'd never discovered what was original and what had been installed by Lomang. Now she knew the truth about the ship's origins, she suspected none of it was Lomang's doing and it was all the peak of Earth's colony ship technology.

"The galactic sector you're from?" Alfie asked. "You mean there's more than one?"

"There are four I'm aware of. There may be more. Humans have been spreading across the galaxy for a long time."

He rubbed his forehead. "It's a lot to take in. I want to believe you. I really do. But if what you're saying is true, how come you're the first to return? And why don't we receive communications from these hundreds of colony worlds? That's what people always say when arguing with Testifiers and, to be honest, I've never had an answer."

"When it comes to habitable planets Earth is in a massive desert. We had to travel a very long way to get here. We've lived ten years on our journey but we've spent even longer in Deep Sleep."

"Deep Sleep? Is that like hibernation? I've read about it."

"We also call it stasis. Basically, the body's functions slow down to a barely perceptible rate. You're alive, but only just, and there's a small but significant death rate. My guess is the colonists who survived the journey didn't want to make the trip back, and they had their work cut out simply surviving and creating a livable world for their offspring. Later generations might not have seen the point in traveling all the way to Earth when other habitable planets were much closer. Or perhaps the Earth's coordinates had been lost. We had a hell of a time finding them."

"But you did." He stared intently into her eyes. "You made the journey. Why? And why haven't I heard about it? The arrival of a starship would be all over the news."

"Would it?" Carina asked. "It seems to me, from what you've said, that people in power don't want to acknowledge there might be human life on other planets."

"There is that, but the *Hangxing Zhe* is huge. There's no hiding her. Someone would have spotted her by now. Are you saying that governments have silenced everyone who's seen her?"

"She's behind the Moon."

"Righhht," he drawled, considering, "but she had to reach the Moon. How did she travel through the Solar System unnoticed?"

Darius had Cloaked her as they neared Earth, but telling Alfie that would complicate matters.

"Look," said Carina, "if you need to be convinced, why not come and see her? We can take you to her right now."

The color drained from his face and his eyes grew round. "Travel to a starship?! Me?"

"We arrived by shuttle but we had to leave it on the edge of the city. Our pilot is waiting there. We can take you to it. Only we can't travel by public transportation. We'll have to walk."

Fortunately, he didn't question the part about avoiding the metro system. "You would take me to your starship behind the Moon? This can't be happening. Wait." He gestured excitedly. "I have to tell some people about this. No one's going to believe me! Can you take more of us? I have some friends in this city. It wouldn't take long—"

"No. Just you. It's too risky to take anyone else."

"Hmm, yeah. I get it." He tapped his nose. "We need to keep this a secret. It's safer that way."

"Exactly. Are you ready to go? Do you need to bring anything?"

"Can I bring an interface?" He rose to his feet.

"It's probably better that you don't have any evidence of what you're about to see." Carina hesitated. "Alfie, I want you to understand, if you come with us you're putting your life at risk. There's a lot I didn't tell you. You'll find out about it soon but first it's important that we convince you we are who we say we are."

"She's deadly serious," Bryce added. "Join up with us and you could die."

"Die?" Alfie sank into his seat. "It's that dangerous?"

"It is," Ferne replied gravely. "We've lost many people over the course of our journey, and not from Deep Sleep Death."

Carina said, "It's only fair that you know. But the reason we're here is because we desperately need the help of someone from Earth, and only an Exodus Testifier would believe us."

"I wouldn't say even *I* completely believe you just yet," said Alfie, "but I'm prepared to keep an open mind. And as to the risks..." His expression hardened with resolve. "All my life I've been laughed at for being a Testifier. I've struggled with jobs, girlfriends, you name it. Nearly everyone I know thinks I'm a crackpot. They're nice enough to my face, but I know that behind my back they talk about me and snigger. Well, here's my chance to prove them wrong. I'm taking it, no matter what might happen. Besides, who would turn down an invitation to visit a freaking starship?! If it's the last thing I ever do, I won't have any regrets."

Though everyone from the *Bathsheba* was tired after their long walk, it was Alfie who was out of breath soon after they set off. He finally took seriously Carina's insistence they avoided public transportation. Naturally, they couldn't Transport to the shuttle with him in tow. He was in poor physical shape and already overly excited. She was worried a sudden introduction to mage powers could give him a heart attack. Moreover, he might be reminded of the General Alert and get spooked.

"But why walk?" he asked, two or three times, puffing and panting. "It's an awfully long way."

Rather than repeat her response that she would explain later yet again, Carina snapped, "We're wanted by the police."

This new information drew him to a halt. "What for? What have you done?" He seemed to be re-thinking his decision.

"We were picked up because we don't have chips."

"Ah, yeah. That makes sense. Okay, foot power it is, but you'll have to slow down. I haven't walked this far since I was a teenager."

He tried to get more information about the *Bathsheba* from them, but Carina shut him down. The risk of being overheard by someone who knew something about their situation was tiny, but also not worth taking.

Poor Alfie was so footsore by the time they reached the place they'd hidden the shuttle he was limping. The vessel was at the bottom of an abandoned quarry, camouflage sheeting echoing the dusty, rocky landscape.

"Where is it?" he asked as they peered over the edge. "I can't see a thing."

"You're not supposed to," said Oriana.

They followed the narrow trail down the quarry's edge. The place was as deserted as it had been when they left it, though there were signs that children came here to play. A circuit for bicycle riders had been recreated from piles of dirt and scrap wood. The sight of it made Carina's heart ache. It was an ordinary, simple construction but for her it symbolized the childhood she and her siblings had never known. Their upbringings had been far from ordinary. She hoped that, one day, their children would play happily somewhere like this, without a care in the world.

"Where is it?" Ferne asked. "I've lost my bearings. I thought Hsiao landed over there."

He pointed, and Carina also couldn't make out the lines of the shuttle. Fear gripped her guts. Was the vessel still here? Or had Castiel found it somehow and taken it?

Lifting her head, she scanned the ridges around the edge of the quarry. They seemed empty.

Alfie had been struggling to catch his breath since they reached the base of the quarry. He squeezed out: "I get it... Very funny. It isn't nice to tease an old man, you know... You really had me going for a while, though, I don't mind admitting."

Bryce had walked ahead of the group. He strode confidently forward until he reached a spot that looked no different from the surrounding area. Reaching up, he rapped with his knuckles, resulting in a hollow, metallic sound. "You're all blind."

Carina sagged with relief and removed her hand from her elixir canister. She'd been convinced they were about to come under attack.

"Thank the stars," said Oriana. "Earth is nice but I can't wait to get back to the ship and have a lovely hot bath."

There was a rustle of shifting sheeting and Hsiao emerged. "Did someone knock?"

"You shouldn't just come out like that," Carina admonished. "What if it had been Castiel?"

"If it had been Castiel I would be dead already. Help me get this sheet off and put away. Your mission was successful I see." She nodded at Alfie, whose jaw looked about to drop from his head.

Due to their repeated experience of applying and removing the camouflage the task was quickly completed. While they worked Alfie simply stood and stared. When it came time to board and return to the *Bathsheba* Nahla called out, "We're ready for you, Mr Binger. Would you step this way?"

He didn't move.

He was weeping.

29

Watching the two Earth men facing off would have been funny if the time remaining to solve the mages' problems hadn't been so tight. Matt and Alfie sat on opposite sides of the mission room, glaring at each other. Van Hasty and Jackson were here too, as well as Bryce, Nahla, and Ava. Somehow, they had to come to a decision about how the coming days would play out. But the Earthers' disagreement was getting in the way.

"You stupid young pup," Alfie said. "You're sitting inside a colony ship and you won't believe the evidence of your own eyes. How much more convincing do you need?"

"It's all fake you gullible old fool. You believe it because you want to believe it. Or maybe you're fake too. Are you part of this? If you are, I warn you you're committing a serious crime. Every single person here will do jail time when this comes out."

"Alfie," Carina said, "whether Matt believes the *Bathsheba* is real is beside the point. We've tried to get his help but he won't take us seriously because he thinks we're tricking him. That's why we've brought you here. We've explained the situation. Can you think of any way you can help us? Is there a person or an organization we can approach who will be able to root out our enemies and eliminate their influence?"

She had three days. Three days until the Black Dogs would fulfill their threat of going down to Earth. Hsiao would take them. After the crisis involving the Obliterator, Carina was in little doubt about it. And if Hsiao refused, Bibik would do it.

The mercs let loose on peaceful Earth would trigger scenarios she cringed to contemplate. Jackson had already killed someone. Wherever they went the Dogs would leave a trail of destruction in their wake. They would wind up dead or permanently incarcerated, destroying the rep of all the *Bathsheba*'s passengers in the process.

Some of them might do okay. The long voyage had tamed some of the Dogs, but the hard core bunch? Their personalities were perfect for survival on the fringes of galactic civilization, but on Earth they were anomalies, incapable of fitting in. It was a difficulty she'd never anticipated, not in all the many times she'd played out in her head their arrival at their destination. She'd become so used to the mercs' behavior and attitudes she hadn't factored it into her planning. Now, they presented as much of a problem as the mages, though an entirely different one.

"It's hard for me to say," Alfie replied after considering for a few moments. "I'm just an ordinary man. I don't have friends in high places. Heck, even my friends don't have friends in high places."

"But you know how things work, right?" asked Carina. "Where I grew up I was a nobody, a street rat, but I could have told you who was pushing the buttons on my planet. My galactic sector was controlled by rival clans, and everyone knew it. The same has to be true everywhere. There have to be people on Earth who hold the real power, people we can approach to fix things without too much bloodshed."

"I told you before," said Matt, "assuming this fantasy you're all playing out was true, approaching those people isn't going to help you. Not if your brother is manipulating them."

"I could suggest a few names," said Alfie. "Maybe that would help."

Matt snapped, "Don't encourage them. You'll only get yourself into trouble. Aiding and abetting a kidnapping is a felony."

"Some names would be a great help," Carina said. "Nahla, could you take notes?" Yet as she spoke a sinking feeling hit in the pit of her stomach. Despite Matt's skepticism he made a good point. The web of Castiel's influence had been woven over decades, with the help of mages. How could she hope to ever tear it down, let alone within three days?

~

ALFIE WANTED to see the Deep Sleep chamber again. He'd already seen them on his first, quick tour of the ship. Carina had felt obliged to show him around a little before springing the reason for his invitation upon him. She hadn't told him about mages yet and she wasn't sure he fully understood their difficulties, but at least he seemed prepared to help.

Hoping she might gain some further insights about Earth from him, Carina agreed to return with him to the chamber. While he peered into an open capsule, she stood in the center of the vast space, recalling the first time she'd set foot on the *Bathsheba*. She and Cadwallader had extracted the security codes to enter the airlocks from Lomang, and she'd used one to open the hatch that led directly to the chamber. The battle with Mezban's soldiers for control of the ship had taken place right here.

"You really spent years inside one of these eggs?" Alfie asked.

"Yep. It isn't as bad as it sounds. You're entirely unconscious. It's like going to sleep and waking up again. It's better for the body to return to consciousness regularly, so we spent years awake too."

"Do you factor the Deep Sleep years into your age? How old are you?"

She shrugged. "It's possible to figure it out but no one bothers."

"Age is just a number. That's how I think about it too." He straightened up, his rotund belly protruding, and ran a hand through his scant hair. "What wouldn't I give to travel across the galaxy? I don't suppose there's a chance you might go back one day?" He grinned cheekily.

"Are you proposing to come with us if we do?"

"Would you have me? I don't know what I could do to earn my passage, but I'd be prepared to do anything. Clean, cook, whatever."

"I'm sorry, Alfie. We won't be going back. It took us so long to get here, and people lost their lives to help us make it. I don't think I could explain it to you properly even if we had time. Your experience of life is so different from mine." *So limited.* How would she even begin to explain about the Sherrerrs, the Dirksens, Lomang and Mezban, the Regians, the mage-controlled society of Magog, or any of the other myriad people and places she'd experienced? His knowledge was limited to one planet.

"What do you mean, *if we had time*?" he asked "You seem to be in a rush to find these people who want to prevent you from settling on Earth. But you're safe enough tucked away behind the Moon. Why are you in a big hurry to fix things?"

"Did you see Jackson and Van Hasty at the meeting just now?"

"The bruisers? I wouldn't like to meet either of *them* in a dark alley."

"They're mercenaries. They helped us get here, and they're my friends. But they're impatient. They want to go to Earth now. If I don't figure something out soon they'll do it and mess everything up."

"Gotcha. You're in a pickle. I hope those names I gave you are useful."

"Thanks," she replied woodenly. "I appreciate it."

"I appreciate you bringing me here. I got the better end of the bargain, that's for sure. What else is there to see on this amazing vessel? I still feel like I'm dreaming but if I am I don't want it to stop."

She took him to the Twilight Dome. Always a show-stopper even for the *Bathsheba*'s long-term passengers, the view thrilled him so much she feared she might have to comm a medic. The sight caused him to collapse into a seat. Eventually, he said, "Why isn't it complete?"

"You mean the transparent overhead? A bomb blew a section out of it. It's the weakest part of the hull."

"A bomb?!"

"If I were to tell you everything that's happened since I first decided I wanted to come to Earth it would take a very long time. Do you want to stay here a while or see more of the ship?"

"I'll stay here," he murmured, transfixed.

"Then I'll see you later. Come and find me when you're ready." She gave him the deck and number of her cabin.

"When do I have to go back to Earth?"

"Have to go back? You don't have to go back. Or not for a while anyway. Do you want to go home?"

"Hell, no. I'm staying as long as you'll have me."

"That's good to hear. It's dangerous for us to go planetside. I'll find somewhere for you to sleep."

"Planetside," he echoed. "I love the sound of that. I could get used to that word."

"See you later, Alfie."

She went to her cabin and was disappointed but not surprised to discover it was empty. She didn't know where Bryce was spending his time these days. She checked her comms but there were no messages from him or anyone else. She didn't know what to do. It was too early to ask Nahla if she'd gotten anywhere with the names Alfie had given her. And if she did get somewhere, how would they even begin to untangle Castiel's web?

She slumped into a chair and put her head in her hands.

30

Each minute of the last two days had dragged past and yet time had also moved at an astonishing speed. Only one day remained until the Black Dog ringleaders would carry out their threat and begin a mass disembarkation of the *Bathsheba*. All Carina's plans, everything she'd done to bring her family to Earth, the sacrifices of the people who had died—it would all come to nothing. She and her siblings would be in a worse situation than they'd been in their home sector. If they'd stayed there they would have been forced to live in secret, but at least they wouldn't have faced the threat of Castiel hunting them down. She wouldn't have had Commander Kee out for her blood.

Van Hasty and Jackson had been subdued around her, as if they felt guilty for the imminent prospect of carrying out their threat. But guilt wouldn't stop them, and nor would the ties of comradeship. At the end of the day, the Dogs were hard-hearted mercenaries. They'd survived their dangerous careers this long because they put themselves first.

Fighting depression and despair, Carina went to see Nahla. She could have talked to her over comm but she yearned to see a friendly, familiar face. Bryce continued to avoid her and she'd been avoiding her other siblings because she felt she'd let them down.

"Hey," said Nahla, with a tone of surprise as Carina walked in. "I didn't expect to see you here."

She hadn't been to her youngest sister's cabin for a long time. Copies of the ancient mage documents covered the walls like strange works of art. Her bed was unmade, sofa cushions were scattered on the floor, and used dishes, mugs, and cutlery sat on the table.

Following Carina's gaze with her own, Nahla seemed to notice these things for the first time.

"It's a mess, right?" she said with some embarrassment. "I'll tidy up."

"Don't bother. I don't mind." Carina moved some clothing aside to sit down. "Are you any further ahead with the names Alfie gave us?"

Nahla had already discovered significant information on the men and women. The Testifier had been correct that they were among the greatest movers and shakers in Earth society and therefore likely to be under Castiel's influence. Yet how to reach them was unclear, or even how to approach the mages manipulating them. It was doubtful that Castiel was doing the work himself. He would have lackeys to take the fall if they were discovered, and there was no telling a mage from a non-mage by outward appearances.

"Umm..." Nahla idly swiped the screen of her interface. "Honestly? No. I've been working on it all night and I managed to access some encrypted comm channels, but it's slow work and I haven't found anything useful. I mean not immediately useful. I found out the head of a media empire is being blackmailed about serious violation of environmental protection laws, and a business mogul made some very odd deals, creating a large profit for a shady company. But—"

"These things would take weeks to get to the bottom of," Carina interrupted.

"Months, perhaps years. It's almost impossible to approach any of these people in person. They have small retinues of highly vetted staff who are the only people they interact with personally on a day-to-day basis. Castiel must have wrangled mages into these teams, but as for telling who they are, and then finding out how our brother is controlling them..." She turned her hands palm upwards in a gesture of helplessness.

"You're saying we might never do it."

"Castiel has decades on us. In a way it's remarkable that his hatred of us runs so deep he would go to all this trouble."

"He always wanted an empire. That was why he betrayed us to the Dirksens. He thought they were his ticket to dominion over a whole galactic sector. Now he has that empire here on Earth. It isn't exactly a sector, but it will do. Making my dream impossible is only a side benefit."

"*Our* dream," Nahla corrected. "It became our dream too somewhere along the way."

Carina reached out and grasped her sister's hand. "Thanks for saying that. I feel as though I dragged you all this way for nothing. I'm sorry the dream didn't come true."

Someone was comming her. She accepted it.

"Hello? Hello?" a voice shouted in her ear. "Can you hear me?"

She winced. "Alfie? Is that you?"

"Ah, good. I've just been given one of your shipboard devices. Wasn't sure if it worked."

"They work the same as they do on Earth. You don't need to raise your voice."

"Ooops, sorry."

"Can I help you?"

Alfie Binger had been enjoying himself immensely in his short time aboard the *Bathsheba*. He'd been seen all over the ship and become everyone's friend. He'd also familiarized himself with every aspect of her layout and had at least a cursory understanding of everything.

"I've been talking to that nice man about your problem. He's explained it in more detail. I'm not sure I quite believe it but my eyes have been opened so much in the last forty-eight hours I think I'm prepared to believe just about anything."

"A nice man? Who have you been talking to?" She imagined it must be Bryce, but Alfie knew his name.

"I think he's called Jackson."

Carina was entirely mystified how Jackson had gone from a 'bruiser' to a nice person in Alfie's estimation, but she couldn't be bothered to go into it. "So you know about mages? Is that what you want to talk about?"

"I'd love to when we have more time, but Jackson said your problem was urgent and you had to find the solution soon. He didn't explain why."

No kidding.

"And I think I have an idea."

She paused. What possible strategy could the man from Earth suggest? He'd only just discovered that mages existed. He couldn't have much understanding of what they could do or the depths of evilness of a Dark Mage like Castiel. Not holding out much hope she said, "Let's hear it."

"Move your ship into Earth orbit. Show the world you exist. Go public. Then go planetside. You'll be celebrities. You'll have the protection of being famous. Your brother won't dare do anything to you."

"Go public?"

Nahla was watching her, hearing only one side of the conversation.

Carina transferred the comm to her cabin's system. "Alfie, can you repeat your idea so my sister can hear it?"

As Nahla listened she met Carina's gaze. She didn't seem to immediately dismiss Alfie's suggestion.

"But will the public even find out we're there?" Carina asked. "My impression is Earth's locked up tight when it comes to the existence of colony ships. A lot of people simply wouldn't believe the evidence, like Matt. Others would be very upset about being proven wrong. So upset they might do something about it. And my brother would do his damnedest to wipe any mention of us from the media."

"That's where the Testifiers come in," said Alfie. "We're all over the place. Every country, every major city in the world. We're in all the businesses, all the professions. Of course, we aren't all out in the open. No one likes being laughed at. But at the last count our official membership stood at over 75,000. And that's only the people who've paid their subs. There are plenty who believe but don't subscribe, and plenty more who are sitting on the fence, but the minute they see images of the *Hangxing Zhe* she'll tip them right off it."

75,000? The reporter who had interviewed him hadn't done his homework. He'd guesstimated 10,000.

Nahla's features brightened with excitement. "The Testifiers would bombard the news stations with images, flood social media, that kind of thing?"

"You got it, and more besides. Send them scenes from the ship's interior. Show them Earth viewed through the Twilight Dome. We'll overload the world with information. The Return of the *Hangxing Zhe* will go viral, and then there'll be no stopping you. Everyone will want to talk to you. You'll be on every talk show, every current affairs program. No station will turn you down because you'll be who their viewers want to see."

"You'll have a platform," Nahla said, eyes shining. "You can explain all about mages and their pacifist culture. You can suggest all the good you could do in the world. And you can set boundaries so you aren't exploited or oppressed. Mages never had a voice before."

"I don't know," said Carina. "The last time mages were out in the open on Earth they were blamed for all the problems and driven offplanet."

"Earth doesn't have most of the problems it had then. What are you going to be blamed for?"

Carina was confident Castiel would think of something.

On the other hand, she didn't have a better idea and they were nearly out of time.

31

"Finally!" Van Hasty exclaimed. "You're finally seeing sense. Shove the Obliterator in their faces, then let's see what they have to say."

"That isn't what this is about," Carina replied. "Not at all." The deck shifted slightly under her feet as Hsiao pulled the *Bathsheba* away from her position on the far side of the Moon.

"Huh?" Van Hasty's lip lifted quizzically. "Then what is it about?"

"It's a publicity exercise."

"It's a what?" The merc turned to Jackson. "Do you know what she's talking about?"

"Beats me. I'm just glad something's happening and we might not be stuck inside this tin can much longer."

"We won't be stuck in here for much longer anyway," Van Hasty replied. "We've only got..." she checked a console "...nineteen hours to go, then Earth is our playground. Man, I can't wait to set foot on solid ground again."

Jackson rolled his shoulders. "I can't wait to find out what new and interesting drinks they serve in Earth bars. Who knows..." he grinned wickedly "...I might even get into a fight."

"Aren't you forgetting something?" Carina asked. "Something about being wanted for murder?"

"A tiny detail. I'm sure you guys will figure it out. You can enchant someone, or whatever it is you do."

"It's called Enthrall and... Never mind."

If mages were to live safely on Earth they couldn't ever do anything outside the law. It wouldn't take much to change public opinion about them. As Bryce had pointed out, mage powers made non-mages feel helpless and inadequate. They would have to tread carefully, and that meant no Enthralling law-enforcers. Jackson's crime was a bridge she would have to cross when she came to it.

Hsiao looked over her shoulder. "You're absolutely sure about this?"

Now you're asking me? The pilot had been more gung-ho about it when under orders from the Black Dogs. "I'm sure."

The bridge door opened and her family poured in, Bryce at their rear.

"We're starting?" Oriana asked. "This is so exciting!"

Carina had outlined Alfie's idea to them and asked for their agreement before trying it out. They'd given it, unsurprisingly. What did they have to lose? "We're going ahead."

"Where's Mr Binger?" Nahla asked.

"He's in a comm room. He wanted a private space to talk with his buddies."

Hsiao said, "Okay, we're out of the Moon's shadow. Anyone on Earth watching this part of the sky is going to see something very interesting."

"Take us there," Carina said.

"Got it. Low-Earth orbit."

The *Bathsheba* would circle the globe, visible even to the naked eye, for as long as it took for people to take notice. Which, Carina guessed, wouldn't be long.

"Better say goodbye to your favorite spots on the ship, kids," said Jackson. He hadn't gotten out of the habit of calling them that even though they were now fully grown. "Earth, here we come."

Alfie comm'd Carina. "The *Hangxing Zhe* has been spotted! It's breaking news on the media stations."

"Good. You've talked to your friends?"

"You better believe it. They're going wild down there. This is gonna be big. The biggest event of my generation. The biggest event in centuries!"

She asked Hsaio to give them a visual. A holo of Earth opened in the center of the bridge. The slowly turning blue and green globe, wreathed in clouds, steadily grew larger. Her heart seemed to beat faster at the same rate the image increased in size. Could Alfie's plan really work? It seemed impossible.

Bryce stood on the opposite side of the bridge. She wished she could go over to him and hold his hand or feel his arm around her as they waited. But the distance between them was more than ordinary space. It was a gulf of differences that she didn't think could ever be spanned.

Alfie was still chattering in her ear, but she'd missed his last few sentences, except that he'd sounded urgent. "What did you say?"

"The Head of the ETA—Exodus Testifiers Association—wants to speak to you. How do I patch her through?"

"Wait a minute. I'll come over there." It was a simpler solution than explaining the comm system. She Transported herself to Alfie's location.

And instantly regretted it.

Alfie turned white as a sheet and clutched his chest. "Where did you come from?! How did you do that?!"

"Sorry, I didn't mean to startle you. I'll talk to the person from your association."

His hand trembling, he turned the mic toward her.

"Hello?" Carina said. "This is Carina Lin of the *Bathsheba*, though you may know her as the *Hangxing Zhe*."

"Hi, Ms Lin. I'm Frankie Longbarrow, representative of the ETA. To say I'm pleased to make your acquaintance is a massive understatement. Alfie's been telling me all about you and your ship. This is going to blow all the Exodus Deniers out of the water. I can't wait to meet you in person. But I should warn you, we're already getting push back from the media. Some respected pundits are saying it's a hoax, a silly stunt, and that your vessel isn't real."

"We thought that might happen. We have someone from Earth

who's actually been living here for several days and even *he* doesn't believe it." And, no doubt, Castiel and his mages were at work getting others to deny the *Bathsheba*'s existence.

"Don't worry, with the images and information Alfie's been sending us, as well as the followers we have all over the world, everyone will have to face the truth of what's in the sky. And as soon as we can get you and your crew down here we'll have living proof to back it up."

"But couldn't they say we're actors?" It was an idea that had just occurred to her.

"Not after we have your genome sequenced. You're descended from people who left Earth thousands of generations ago. Your DNA will prove it."

"Right." Giving up her DNA wasn't something she'd anticipated. It almost certainly held the secret to her magehood, and so it could be used to identify other mages within the population. Yet if they were to win public trust they had to be transparent. "I'll have to think about that."

"Fine, fine," said Frankie. "One step at a time. We mustn't get ahead of ourselves. This is amazing! I can't believe it's happened in my lifetime. I feel like this generation is the luckiest alive. So are you in a way. Several tech companies have approached the Association for confirmation that a colony ship really has returned. They'll give their eye teeth plus a lot of money for access to everything on your vessel."

"I hadn't thought of that angle."

"There will be many angles no one thought of popping up over the next few days. When will you be able to come to the surface? Alfie says you have a shuttle and he's flown in it, the lucky devil."

"We're going to sit tight for a day and see how things pan out. How does that sound?"

"Whatever you say. You're the one calling the shots. We'll keep up the pressure on the media, academia, and businesses down here. You can leave everything in the ETA's hands."

"Thanks. I should go and see what's happening on the ship."

"No, thank *you*. It's a privilege to meet you, Carina Lin."

To avoid giving Alfie another turn, Carina stepped out of the comm room before Transporting to the bridge. Everything was much as she'd left it. Her siblings had spread out around the space and Earth had grown so large it occupied the entire holo.

"Entering orbit in three minutes fifty," said Hsiao. "What's happening planetside?"

"A war of opinion from the sound of it. Castiel is trying to erase the knowledge of our existence from public consciousness and the Testifiers are forcing the *Bathsheba* down their throats."

"Who's gonna win, I wonder?" Bryce asked softly.

Van Hasty said, "You know the Obliterator's still an option, right? Wouldn't take a minute to blast Castiel's base to smoke and ashes."

"If you remember, there's the small matter of the hundreds of other people we would kill," Carina countered. When Van Hasty seemed unmoved she added, "And Castiel might not be there anymore. If he has any sense he will have left the second we flew out of the cover of the Moon."

Van Hasty shrugged. "Maybe. But it would send a message."

"Exactly the kind of message I don't want to send. I don't get why that's so hard for you to understand." Carina despaired of ever re-focusing certain mercs' minds away from violence.

She watched Earth's surface, oceans and continents moving slowly past. They were approaching with the sun at their backs. In galactic terms the planet wasn't old but intelligent life there was—the oldest human life in the galaxy, some said. It was certainly the origin planet of mages. Had those who had fled persecution ever imagined that one day their descendants would return?

She thought of the mages she'd left behind. Did the Council still exist? Magda, the Spirit Mage had died saving Jace's life, and Justin had been murdered by Castiel. How would the young mages be Summoned to a Matching without their Spirit Mage? How would they meet, marry, and have children, when they lived secretly, often hidden even from each other?

Taking Darius from them had weighed on her conscience, but she didn't regret it. A seven-year-old couldn't bear responsibility for the destiny of all the mages in a sector. It was too much to ask, no matter the consequences.

"The *Bathsheba* is in Earth orbit," Hsiao announced.

Whoops and hollers of celebration followed.

An alarm blared out, cutting through the noise. The voices stuttered to silence until only the alarm could be heard.

"What the hell?" Van Hasty breathed in disbelief, looking up from an interface. "Hull breach. Deck Four."

"Have we been fired on?" Carina asked. "Hsiao, any sign of ships on the long range scanners?"

She consulted her screen. "Not a thing."

"I don't understand. What about an attack from the surface?"

"No way. We would have picked it up."

"Then...?" She turned hopelessly to Van Hasty, who stared intently at her console.

The alarm blared on, unremitting.

Carina comm'd the Dogs, sending a breach team to Deck Four. The *Bathsheba* would self-repair eventually, but a hull breach was too risky to leave unattended.

"Another breach!" yelled Van Hasty. "Deck Two."

But how?

Open-mouthed shock permeated the bridge.

"Should I take us out of orbit?" Hsiao asked.

"I don't know. Stand by." Carina consulted the data from the ship's sensors for herself. There was nothing to indicate they'd been fired upon. No record of a burst of energy in their vicinity or traces of an after-effect.

"Breach on Deck Seven," Van Hasty snapped. "It's the Dome."

The *Bathsheba* seemed to be splitting apart of her own volition.

Splitting apart.

"It's Split!" Carina exclaimed. "Castiel is Casting Split on the ship."

"That can't be it," said Parthenia. "The *Bathsheba* is far too large to be affected by Split. When he used it on Ostillon it only worked on shuttlecraft."

"But it isn't only Castiel," Ferne retorted gravely. "He has all the mages on Earth working with him."

32

T he noise of the alarm bounced around inside Carina's skull, growing louder and louder. She realized it wasn't only the alarm she was hearing but voices yelling as the debate about what to do grew more and more heated.

"Shut up!" she screamed. "Shut up! I can't hear myself think!"

The voices quietened.

"Turn off that goddamned alarm too. We know what's happening."

Reports of more breaches had flooded in. The bridge was sealed off and everyone else on the ship was wearing EVA suits due to the threat of depressurization.

Silence fell, but it was short-lived.

Van Hasty got up in Carina's face. "We need to fire the Obliterator, now! We're not taking this attack lying down."

"Fire it on what? The thousands of mages dotted all over the planet? If you fire that thing you'll kill thousands of civilians."

"Maybe it'll make your sick shit of a brother step down."

"He won't care. He'll blame us, and rightly. We'll be the ones firing. No one on Earth understands about mages. They won't know we were trying to defend ourselves."

"Damn it, Lin!" Van Hasty spat. "What happened to you? You lost your guts somewhere along the way."

"I didn't lose anything. I gained something—the ability to think before I acted. Now back off!"

Van Hasty stepped away, glaring.

"We could try Repulse," Oriana suggested.

"Against thousands of mages?" Carina shook her head. "Even Darius couldn't fend off that many Casts all at once."

"I could try," he said.

"It would exhaust you and we need you as our last line of defense."

"The Dogs can't keep pace with the breaches," Hsiao reported. "We need to think about evacuation."

"To the surface?" asked Carina. "Where Castiel has a welcoming party?"

"I can Cloak the shuttle," said Darius.

"I hate to mention it," Hsiao said, "but it won't accommodate more than half the passengers, and at the rate the hull is disintegrating there won't be time for a second trip."

Decide who is to go and who will stay, awaiting the Bathsheba's *destruction? Who could make those choices?*

Parthenia said, "Whoever goes to Earth might be able to hide from Castiel for some time, providing he doesn't know where the shuttle lands. Perhaps we could draw lots. Little Carina and Ava must go, naturally."

Carina had almost forgotten about Ava's daughter, her namesake. Her throat constricted and she swallowed the lump that had formed there.

"And Officer Matt and Alfie Binger," Parthenia continued. "This isn't their fight."

"Alfie!" Carina exclaimed. "I'd forgotten all about him." She comm'd the Earth man. "I need you to tell me what reports are coming from Earth. Has there been any news on the state of the ship?"

"Ah, that's what all that clamor was about. Thank goodness it stopped. It was giving me a headache."

"Alfie," she repeated, "what's the news from Earth about the *Bathsheba*?"

"An awful lot of debate about her existence, but the believers seem to be winning. According to Ms Longbarrow some wonderful images of her have appeared on all the news channels."

"Nothing about her breaking up?"

"Breaking up?!"

"Sorry, try not to worry about it. Just... stay where you are, okay? Don't leave that room."

The door would seal if the adjoining passageway depressurized.

She cut the comm. "No one on Earth knows what's happening. I guess the breaches aren't immediately obvious, especially when most people have never seen a starship."

Parthenia said, "So the *Bathsheba* will fall apart and tumble from the sky, and Castiel's people will be able to play it off as if she never existed."

"Something like that," Carina muttered.

"And if any of us survive," said Ferne, "he can hunt us at his leisure."

"At least three breaches on all decks," Hsiao reported. "Decks Four through Seven fully depressurized."

"Lin!" Van Hasty barked. "Time's up. Make a decision or I will."

The deadly peril everyone aboard faced pressed in on Carina like the atmosphere of a high-grav planet. She struggled to breathe as fears hammered her mind, destroying her thought processes.

"I *wish* we had a way to Send to all those mages," Oriana pined. "If only we could talk to them and explain who we are and why we're here."

"Castiel must have fed them a bunch of lies," said Ferne, "or he's put them in fear of their lives if they don't do what he says."

Nahla said, "More likely he's put them in fear of someone else losing their life—someone they love. That's how he operates."

"But if they all stood up to him at once," said Oriana, "he would have no choice but to back down. He can't defend himself against all of them at the same time."

Ferne sighed. "There's no point in wishing. We don't know those people. We don't have any of their personal items. How could we Locate them among Earth's millions?"

Carina sucked in a great gulp of air. "We *can* Send to them. Darius can do it!"

"But how?" Oriana asked. "He doesn't have—"

"He doesn't need anything to Locate them. He's a Spirit Mage. He can Summon them."

A pause followed. Everyone was still.

Jackson frowned. "He can *what*?"

"Do it, Darius," Carina urged, adding, "Do you remember how? You do know how to Summon, right?" Anxiety gnawed at her stomach as he blinked, thinking.

He'd only spent a few weeks with the old mage, Magda. The long days he'd attended lessons in her tent had made Carina angry at the time. She'd been jealous of the woman's influence on her brother and considered the expectations she had of him too great. But now she prayed with all her heart that Magda had taught him the Cast that only Spirit Mages could perform.

"I-I think so," he quietly replied. "I'd forgotten about it until you mentioned it. I recall learning the Cast but I never had a chance to practice it. This will be my first time."

"Oh, you have to reach them, Darius," said Oriana. "Tell them mages are aboard the ship they're destroying, as well as lots of innocent people. Ask them to please stop. And tell them Castiel is a Dark Mage who will hurt them. Tell them we have another way for them to live, that they won't have to hide anymore."

"That's rather a lot," Darius nervously quipped.

Carina took her canister of elixir from her belt and set it down in front of him. "In case you need extra."

Parthenia, Oriana, and Ferne did the same.

Nahla kissed his cheek. "Good luck."

Darius looked from face to face, unscrewed the lid of his elixir bottle, and drank.

Carina caught Bryce's gaze. Making eye contact with him broke the dam and her tears flooded out. The last thing she wanted was for her youngest brother to carry the responsibility of saving everyone's lives, but they were out of options. She sank into a seat, wretched with despair.

All attention in the bridge was on Darius. Even Hsiao had ceased monitoring her screens. The young man's eyes were shut tight and his brow furrowed with concentration. Beads of sweat erupted on his forehead. His lips moved silently.

It was working. He was talking to the other mages.

A scene from a long time ago popped into Carina's mind: a little boy with a mop of dark hair mentally conversing with a starwhale, a living creature that flew between stars, asking it how it was doing, and entirely forgetting the important part of the message.

Darius would not forget this time.

Without opening his eyes, he blindly reached for another canister of elixir. Oriana snatched one up and thrust it into his hands.

He drank more elixir. The beads of sweat on his forehead coalesced and ran down his face. His skin paled and the line between his brows deepened. His shoulders lifted and fell as his chest heaved.

Hsiao swiveled to consult her screens, and then turned back to face Darius.

Carina didn't dare ask if her brother's efforts were having an effect. She didn't want to break his concentration.

Halfway through his fourth canister of elixir, his eyes opened. Instantly, he collapsed, flopping forward, propping his elbows on his knees while his head hung low. Carina stepped to his side and gently touched his shoulder.

"It's done," he whispered.

She looked to Hsiao for confirmation.

The pilot nodded, a grin wreathing her face. "No more breaches."

"Thank the stars!" Oriana exclaimed. "That was fantastic, Darius."

Nahla smiled. "You always were my hero."

But Darius was beyond hearing them. He looked utterly spent.

"Jackson," said Carina, "could you coordinate the repairs?"

"Copy. That kid's a marvel."

It went without saying.

Though she hardly dared believe it, a small flame of hope flared in Carina's chest. If Darius could speak to all Earth's mages, albeit at great expense of energy, there was a chance they could defeat Castiel. A Dark Mage could not Summon, and they would already be afraid of him. He couldn't hide his true nature for very long.

And the Testifiers were working to make sure he couldn't cover up the arrival of the *Bathsheba* with her friendly mages, here to do good and help humankind. Though things had looked dicey for a while, the publicity stunt had worked.

"Someone's hailing us from the surface," Van Hasty said. "Won't give his name. Says Carina will know who he is."

The flame of hope flickered and threatened to go out.

"It's Castiel," said Oriana.

"No," Carina said, "I don't think it is. Put him on general comm."

"Ms Lin. I felt confident we would meet again one day. I'm glad you made it here. It's quite the journey, isn't it?"

"What do you want? Spit it out."

"Castiel and I are impressed by your ability to persuade the mages to halt their Split Casts. We concede defeat. You've won. I expect we'll see you on the surface soon."

"Not if I see you first, Kee." She gestured to Van Hasty, drawing her finger across her throat.

The merc closed the comm. "Kee? That rings a bell."

"Commander Kee of the Dirksens. He's the one who helped Castiel get here."

"He must like him a lot."

"He probably despises him, but he loved Sable Dirksen."

Van Hasty grimaced. "Ugh. Awkward."

"Do you believe the bit about them conceding defeat?" Ferne asked.

"Not for a second, but, nevertheless, it's time to go planetside."

33

As the shuttle conveyed them to the planet surface, Carina asked Oriana to switch places so she could sit next to Parthenia.

As she settled in next to her oldest sister, Parthenia side-eyed her. "You want to talk to me?"

"I've been thinking about this publicity tour the Testifiers have set up." The group had become the mages' de facto agents, arranging interviews with all the major media channels and booking their transportation and hotels. It turned out some rather rich individuals were Testifiers, and they were very happy to pay to be proved right. Everything seemed to be working as Alfie had suggested. They were already famous all over the globe. If anything happened to them hard questions would be asked in high places.

"What about it?"

"I want you to take the lead in representing the mages."

"But you're the oldest and, to be frank, this was all your idea. The journalists will want to talk to the leader of our expedition, not the foot soldiers."

"You were always more than a foot soldier, but that isn't the reason I'm asking you. You will be way better at giving interviews than me, and you'll give a better impression of mages and what we stand for."

"What?" Parthenia turned to face her. "What are you talking about?"

"You carry yourself like a queen, Parthenia. You always have. And you speak really well. Sometimes I think you have a thesaurus in your head. You know when to speak plainly and when to shut up. If an interviewer got on my nerves I might run my mouth and say something I shouldn't. Basically, you grew up in a wealthy family while I was a slum brat, and it shows."

"Hmpf. Well, I'm sure Father would be delighted that my lessons in comportment, rhetoric, and oratory paid off."

"Will you do it?"

Parthenia looked out of the window. The black of space was transforming to the crystalline blue of a cloudless sky. "What exactly do we want to tell the world about mages? This has happened so fast I haven't had time to think about it."

"I wondered about that too, but it's easy. You just need to tell them what Jace would have said, about how we don't believe in using our powers to control or hurt people, or even to gain an advantage. That we want to help people." Carina swallowed and added, "That was how my dad and Ma were trapped. Did you know? I'm not sure if I ever told you."

"No, you never did."

Though the story involved Stefan Sherrerr, Carina tried to keep him out of it as much as she could as she explained how Ba had wanted to help people trapped by an earthquake, and that was how he and Ma had been exposed.

Parthenia listened solemnly and didn't speak when Carina had finished.

She continued, "You were close to Jace and spent more time with him than anyone else. He knew mage culture inside out. If you're ever in any doubt about the answer to a question you only need to ask yourself what would Jace say? But you have to be careful about the General Alert. What you'll be saying will sound awfully like what the public has been told to watch out for. You'll need to spin it so it's clear mages aren't anything to do with that. You should question it, ask where it's from and who's behind it. When they can't answer they'll look stupid and stop asking about it. Hopefully, the Alert will fade from public consciousness."

After a pause, Parthenia murmured, "I suppose I could do it."

"Oriana and Ferne could help, and so could Nahla. Though she isn't a mage she could talk about what it's like growing up as a non-mage in a mage family. People will be interested to hear about that. You have to emphasize that mages aren't better than non-mages, only different. We can make them feel inadequate, you see. That's what Bryce told me."

"*That's* what he's upset about?"

"Yes."

"What about Darius?"

"Darius and I..." Carina glanced over her shoulder and caught his gaze. He'd been watching and listening the whole time "...we have other work to do."

"And Bryce? He knows what it's like living with mages too."

"I have no idea about Bryce plans."

A SEA of expectant faces awaited them on Earth. Bibik landed the shuttle at an airport in the main city of the most powerful country, according to the Testifiers. It was a place called New Tunka, capital of Ballarkland. They hadn't been here on any of their previous, clandestine visits. Carina took a moment before stepping out of the shuttle to take in the view. The city beyond the airport boundaries looked more built up than other metropolises she'd seen, such as Alfie's, and definitely way more built up than the small town Matt was from.

Officer Matt was behind her waiting to disembark. His superiors had agreed to waive kidnapping charges, accepting there had been a 'misunderstanding'. Ava was with him and so was little Carina. Alfie had elected to remain on the *Bathsheba*, unsurprisingly. It would have taken a crow bar to lever him from the ship, despite her recent brush with destruction.

New Tunka spread out to the horizon, or at least it seemed to spread out. Like everywhere else Carina had seen on Earth, the greenery of the city made it hard to distinguish what was town and what was country. No building stood higher than three stories, and no motorized vehicles ran along the roads.

"Umm..." said Oriana, standing behind her.

"Sorry." She took a step forward, but something buzzed into her field of vision. She swiped it, knocking the buzzing thing off course. "What the hell's *that*?"

"It's a camera drone, moron," Van Hasty yelled from somewhere back in the line. "Move your ass, Carina. Some of us want to get a look at Earth."

The drone returned, swooping in front of her face again. She frowned at it angrily, but then, remembering this was the first sight of a mage for most Earth citizens—that they knew about—she forced her frown away and waved at the reporters.

Despite the extreme unlikelihood of Castiel Splitting her in front of the world's media, she couldn't help tensing, fearing attack, as she descended from the shuttle.

"No camouflage sheet this time," Oriana whispered.

"Be careful," Carina warned. "I know this looks safe, but..."

"Don't worry. I know my brother well."

A barrier encircled the shuttle exit, preventing the reporters from approaching too close. Men in uniform stood inside it. One beckoned her. As she stepped forward, a barrage of questions began.

"How does it feel to arrive on Earth?"

"Where are you from? What's the name of your planet?"

"Are you one of the mages? Which of you can do magic?"

"How long did it take to get here?"

"Have you seen aliens? Is there intelligent life on other worlds?"

"What are your plans now you've arrived?"

Carina smiled but didn't answer. Apparently, the rights to the 'first interview with the returning colonists' had been signed away for a very large sum.

"Ms Lin? Ms Lin!"

She looked for the person calling her name so insistently. A florid, middle-aged woman in a thick coat was pressed up against the barrier, waving wildly. "They won't let me through," she called out as they made eye contact.

"Frankie Longbarrow?"

"That's right. We finally meet, haha."

"Please let this woman in," Carina asked one of the uniformed men. "She's, uh, part of my media team."

"I thought it was you," Frankie said breathlessly after ducking under the barrier. "Alfie described you to me very well."

Carina didn't ask what he'd said. "Thanks for all the ETA's help. We could never have done this without you."

"It's our pleasure."

The endless yelled questions continued as they crossed the open space to the nearest building.

"I need to discuss your itinerary in detail," said Frankie. "It's complicated. You're going to be very busy for the next few months until things die down."

"Actually, my sister will be the main person handling the interviews."

"Oh?" Frankie's eyebrows rose and she craned her neck, looking backward. "Which one is she?"

"You'll soon spot her. We look very alike."

"So you're handing her the reins? I understand. You have plenty else to do."

They'd arrived at the building. The doors were open and the interior looked invitingly empty and quiet. Carina wondered if she was being selfish in asking Parthenia to present mages to the world. She couldn't deny the thought of being famous and under constant scrutiny appalled her. But her reasoning was also valid. Her oldest sister was perfectly suited to the task, whereas she was more of a behind-the-scenes person.

Before entering the building, she took a look at the line of shuttle passengers, stretching back to the vessel. Oriana, Ferne, and Ferne's latest girlfriend, who came from Marchon, walked in a little group. Matt had his arm around Ava and she was holding her daughter's hand. Parthenia and Darius followed them, looking somewhat apprehensive. Van Hasty and Rees strode behind the pair, towering a head taller. They were unarmed, at Carina's request, and didn't appear too happy about it. Nahla was with her merc partner, a man a little younger than her and far less aggressive than most of the Dogs. About halfway back walked Chi-tang and Cheepy, bizarrely lovey-dovey now they'd arrived at their destination.

The line continued on, men and women who had taken part in the long journey. In the many years of the voyage she'd come to know them all by name. They'd eaten and socialized together. There had been fallings out and reconciliations, anger, despair, and tears, laughter, joy, and delight. Soon, they were to part ways. Things would never be the same again. Everyone would create a life on Earth, get jobs, have families, put down roots. She wondered how their lives would turn out.

She had a feeling she would never know.

34

Carina waited two weeks before going after Castiel. Though the Testifiers did an excellent job of guarding or destroying anything personal to the mages, realistically it was only a matter of time before their ranks were infiltrated and the Dark Mage would Transport his siblings to his side. As long as he lived, they would be under constant threat of disappearing, never to be seen again.

Over those two weeks a great outpouring of data had been going on from the *Bathsheba* to Earth scientists. Her logs, schematics, every bit of information about her systems and all the devices aboard. Tech companies had started a bidding war for priority access to the ship but the consensus among her passengers was they did not want to profit from her, that her tech should benefit humanity as a whole. After all, the vessel hadn't belonged to them in the first place.

"You're going to kill him?" Parthenia asked before Carina set off.

"Don't you think he deserves to die after everything he's done?"

"Yes, but..."

"I know Ma wouldn't want me to do it, but she would also want me to protect all of you. I can't do both, and it's better that I do it than one of his full siblings. I can live with myself afterward. I'm not sure you can."

"I've always hated killing. Even the Regians. You're right. I don't know if I could bring myself to kill Castiel."

"I know. It's one of the things I like about you." *One of the things I'm going to miss.*

"Darius is going too? I saw him getting ready."

"I'd rather not take him but I'm going to need him."

"And Bryce?"

"He doesn't know about it."

"You two *still* aren't talking? That's ridiculous. You're both being stubborn."

"It isn't stubbornness. I'd be happy to patch things up. He isn't interested. He's moved on. He'll find a nice non-mage partner on Earth. He has millions to choose from."

"No, he won't. Bryce has been through thick and thin with you. He won't be happy with anyone else. You two are made for each other."

"I thought so too, once. But I pushed him too far and now I don't think he can ever come back."

"He will. He just needs time."

Carina doubted it but she didn't bother arguing. She had an important job to do.

NEAR THE ANCIENT mage hideaway in the mountains, all was still. Even the ever-present wind had dropped to nothing and a hot sun baked the rocks. As Darius brought the mercs in, they quickly took stock of their surroundings.

"Where did you stash the equipment, Lin?" Pamuk asked.

Carina nodded to the dip in the slope where she'd put the armor, rifles, and other equipment she'd Transported down from the *Bathsheba*.

"I still say we should blow that place from orbit," Jackson grumbled.

"Yeah, 'cause no one's going to notice, right?" Carina asked sarcastically.

"Quit with the stupid suggestions, Jackson," said Van Hasty. "This might be our last chance for a fight and I'm gonna take it. Shit, Earth's boring. I've never known such a peaceful planet. Even Magog was more interesting."

"You didn't come with us to Magog," said Carina.

"Exactly."

The rest of the mercs were retrieving weapons and donning armor. Carina and Darius suited up too.

"Do you feel him close by?" she asked her brother over comm.

"Yes, he's already here."

Whether Castiel had set watchers who had spotted their arrival or if the mountain was his permanent abode wasn't clear, but Carina's intuition about where she would find her half-brother had been correct.

"Are we Transporting in?" asked Jackson, "or assaulting from outside?"

"There's only one entrance I know of and it's only one man wide. I want you to take a team, scout it out, and assess the level of defense. Remain outside to catch anyone trying to escape, and await orders."

"What do we do with them if they come out?"

"If they surrender take them prisoner."

"What if it's your brother or Kee?"

"Kill on sight."

Allowing either man to live was too risky.

She could only Transport mercs to the areas she'd been inside the mountain, and they were only a small portion of the whole. But it couldn't be helped. With luck they would have the element of surprise and would quickly mow down the opposition. She hoped that, on this peaceful world, their soldiers only comprised the men and women who had partaken in their galactic journey and there were few recruits from the local population.

She didn't anticipate encountering many mages. From the ones who had come forward and revealed themselves, she understood that Castiel's main method of persuasion had been convincing them that non-mages would hate and persecute them. The reception Carina and her siblings had received put the lie to his assertions and much of his support had melted away. Yet, no doubt, there were also mages he was controlling by more nefarious means. She and Darius would have to be on their guard.

"Ready?" she asked him.

"Yes."

She began to Cast. As soon as the Dogs had gone in, she Transported herself and Darius to the great chamber with the waterfall.

Already, flashes of pulse fire could be seen lighting up the exits, though their hiss couldn't be heard over the roar of the waterfall. She dragged her brother to the side of the chamber, where a protrusion gave a little cover. The cavern seemed empty, the only movement the ripples of the pond where falling water crashed into it.

"He's here!" Darius exclaimed.

She couldn't see Castiel but she didn't doubt her brother's words.

She switched her comm to external. "Castiel! Your plan has failed. We've won. You have two choices: leave Earth forever or face the consequences of your actions."

Castiel's voice floated back, thin and faint, "The consequences of *my* actions? As I recall, it wasn't I who murdered my father. It wasn't I who executed Sable Dirksen in cold blood, condemning her to a horrible fate without even the justice of a fair trial."

"They earned their deaths, the same as you'll earn yours if you don't get off this planet."

"Even if I agreed with you, I am sadly unable to comply. The starship we arrived on was destroyed long ago. So unless you plan on giving me yours..."

He was stalling. Castiel would never agree to her terms even if she put the *Bathsheba* in his hands. The immediate area was clear. She scanned upward. The walls were smooth, impossible to scale. There was the possibility that Castiel could Transport soldiers in—

Something was moving within the waterfall. The endless rush of water had scooped a hollow behind it. She fired. The soldier fell without a sound, tumbling down and disappearing into the pool.

"I see your aim has improved," said a voice.

Kee was here too.

"I had a lot of time to practice."

Castiel needed a line of sight to attempt to Split them, and they had good visibility. No one could sneak up on them. They could survive here a long time and Transport out within a few seconds, but that wasn't the point.

"Darius," she comm'd, one to one, "we have to find them."

While the exchange had been going on within the chamber, the fighting outside had intensified. An enemy soldier stumbled through one of the entrances, fell down face forward, and was still.

"I know," her brother replied.

"They must be on the far side of the pool. It's the only spot we can't see."

"I'll Transport us."

"No, I'll do it. I want you to conserve your elixir. And remember your promise, right?"

"I remember."

Before they'd embarked on the mission, she'd made him swear that if she was killed he had to leave. He would need elixir to do it and she didn't want him to run out. She comm'd Van Hasty, who was somewhere within the depths of the mountain.

"Copy," the merc replied. "I know where you are. The place with the waterfall, right? Stay put until I get there. Resistance is heavy but we're breaking through."

They waited, watching for signs of another attempt to reach them. Castiel would be growing impatient, and he was undoubtedly receiving the news that his troops were being defeated.

A comm arrived from Van Hasty. "We're in. Where are you?"

Carina Cast.

As they arrived it took her a second to get her bearings. Three figures stood under an overhang, armored up. She turned to the entrance.

It was empty.

Where was Van Hasty?

A pulse round flashed. Darius gasped. He'd been hit.

She fired back and grabbed her brother's arm, hauling him toward the gap in the wall. More pulses flashed past. Kee was firing and perhaps Castiel too, though that had never been his style. The third person had to be his daughter. Perhaps she was the other one shooting at them.

"He's Casting," breathed Darius. There was a gulp as he drank elixir.

While Darius was Casting Repulse against Castiel he was defenseless. Carina pushed him behind the entrance, but soldiers were running down the passageway. They were not Dogs. She shot at the three armored figures in the cavern, spraying them with fire, then focused on the approaching soldiers.

White-hot heat exploded at her neck. She'd been hit. She fought down a shriek and struggled to hold onto her rifle. Her suit's analgesics kicked in, forcing the painkiller through her skin, and the agony faded. But the scent of her burned flesh told her it was a serious wound. She had to Cast Heal but there was no time. She needed a reprieve. She would Cast Transport instead and get them out of the fighting for a short while.

She sucked on the tube leading to her suit's reservoir, but no elixir spurted into her mouth. The pulse round had destroyed the tube. "Darius..."

He was on his knees. He'd taken another hit, and he couldn't defend himself because he was too busy Casting against Castiel.

Where were the mercs? There had to be another cavern with a waterfall somewhere in the mountain and Van Hasty had gone there.

The enemy soldiers had nearly reached them. She shot into their midst. One fell, but the others rushed up, grabbed her, and threw her down.

THEY'D TAKEN off her armor. Darius knelt beside her, also without his suit.

Castiel, Kee, and Letitia had removed their helmets.

Kee had aged significantly. His cheeks were sunken in and his eyes sat deep in their sockets, but they were as dark and intelligent as ever.

"Carina Lin," he said softly. "If I'd known you would kill Sable one day, you would never have left the interrogation cell alive."

"Strange that you would feel so strongly about such a terrible person, Kee." She winced as pain lanced her neck. "Was it really worth devoting your life to getting revenge for a monster?"

"You have no idea of the depths and richness of her personality. You did the galaxy a great disservice when you deprived it of her presence. It's long past time for a reckoning."

"*Long* past time," Castiel agreed, "for that and many other things."

"I don't know what you hope to achieve by killing us," Carina said defiantly. "You've lost the mages under your control. Parthenia will turn Earth into somewhere they can live without fear. Your time here is over, whether we live or not."

"You underestimate the great satisfaction your deaths will bring me regardless, and you overestimate Parthenia's abilities. Though she may persuade the public not to hate her, she will have *my* hatred for the rest of her life, which I aim to cut short as soon as I have the opportunity."

"Don't do it," said Darius. "We're family. You and I are brothers. We grew up together. For a long time, I looked up to you. You can still change, Castiel. You don't have to do this."

He chuckled. "Sweet little Darius. Mother's darling. How I hated you from the very minute you were born, before anyone even knew what a powerful mage you were. Ferne and Oriana were always stupid but tolerable. You, however, were something else. I knew for a long time I couldn't allow you to exist."

"I'm sorry," Carina whispered.

Darius bowed his head. "You don't have anything to be sorry for, sis."

"How sweet," said Castiel. "I would so love to make a great display of your deaths, to show the world what should be done to those evil arrivals from the stars. But, though it pains me to say it, your soldiers are closing in. We must make quick work of this and then retreat to a safer spot."

"What about you?" Carina asked, lifting her gaze to the woman at his side, who hadn't said a word during the entire exchange.

Letitia looked away.

Now Carina could get a good look at her, the likeness of the woman to Ma struck her more forcefully than ever. Tears of grief sprang to her eyes. *I did my best, Ma. I tried my best to save them.*

"Weeping won't help you," said Castiel. "You won't find any mercy here."

"Is this what you want?" Carina asked Letitia.

"How dare you address my daughter?" Castiel demanded. "Be silent. Kee, do the honors. Carina is yours and I get to kill Darius, as we agreed."

Kee lifted his rifle.

"He hates you," Carina said to Letitia. "You know that, right? You've always known it." She launched herself at Kee, head-butting him in the stomach.

Winded, the old man landed heavily.

A flash of light lit up the dim space. Someone had fired. As Carina struggled on the ground with Kee, she yelled, "Letitia, come over to our side! You can live freely as a mage." Sounds of a fight were coming from one side but she couldn't make out what was happening. "You'll never please him!" she shouted. "He'll hate you forever."

Kee was under her. She drove her knee into his chin. There was the crack of shattering teeth and blood ran from between his thin lips.

A second flash ignited in the cavern.

Kee's grip on his rifle loosened. She wrested it from his grasp and spun it around. The old commander raised his hands as if to ward her off.

She fired.

Kee was no more.

She turned.

Darius was down.

Dead?

The horrible scent of burned flesh was rank in the atmosphere.

A little way off were two figures, one kneeling, the other standing. Carina squinted at them she crawled to her brother.

"Don't do it, darling," Castiel pleaded. "You know I love you."

"It isn't true!" Carina yelled. She touched Darius. He was warm but that didn't mean anything, and with their suits gone she had no elixir. "You *know* the truth, Letitia. You know it."

The woman's head swiveled toward Carina's.

Their gazes met.

She turned back to her father and shot him in the head.

35

She Healed Darius with Castiel's elixir. From what Darius said when he came around, Castiel had shot him but at the last millisecond Letitia had pushed her father. The round couldn't have quite hit its mark or Carina wouldn't have been able to bring Darius back.

Letitia and Castiel must have been the pair she'd heard fighting. Eventually, the daughter had got the upper hand, and with the truth of Carina's words ringing in her ears, she'd delivered the coup de grâce. Then it was only a matter of waiting for the Black Dogs to complete their mission. The hostiles Carina had shot at had been forced away to deal with the mercs under Van Hasty's command.

They left Castiel and Kee's corpses in the cavern. Neither of them deserved a decent burial, and though their presence besmirched the ancient place, the mages who had lived there had departed millennia ago. It was only a deserted cave in the mountains.

The long story of the Dark Mage's hatred for his family was finally over. They could live in peace, which in some ways made Carina's delivery of her decision even harder. After several days of gathering courage, she explained what she intended and her reasoning, adding, "It has to be this way. I'm sorry."

"No, it doesn't!" Parthenia sobbed, trembling with shock. "You can't do it. I couldn't bear it."

Oriana simply wailed, unable to verbalize her sorrow.

Darius hung his head.

"Is this what you want?" Ferne asked him quietly.

He nodded. "Carina's right."

Nahla turned away, running her fingertips under her eyes.

Parthenia asked, "Does Bryce know about this?"

"I haven't told him," Carina replied. She hadn't seen any reason to.

"Then *I* will. I bet he'll have something to say about it."

"Whatever he has to say, it won't change my decision."

Ever since asking Darius to use the Summon Cast to speak to the mages on Earth, the fate of the mages they'd left behind had weighed heavily on her conscience. They had no Spirit Mage, no way of coming together, and their lives were already hard and dangerous. If she could return to her sector with Darius and find them, she could tell them about Earth, the safe haven for mages. They could build colony ships and, one day, arrive at a true home for themselves and their descendants.

"You'll take the *Bathsheba*?" Ferne asked solemnly.

"Everything about her has been downloaded to some place or another on Earth. If someone wants to build another colony ship they can. They don't need a model to copy."

"But you can't fly her alone," Parthenia protested. "She's massive. It's impossible."

"I know I can't do it alone. Hsiao and some of the Black Dogs have agreed to come along. I got their agreement before I told you."

"No way!" Ferne exclaimed. "They only just got here."

"They don't like Earth," Carina explained.

"Don't like it?" Oriana squeaked. "What's not to like? Earth's lovely."

"They've spent most of their lives aboard starships and fighting battles. There's nothing for them here. And if Jackson stays he's going to prison."

She recalled asking Hsiao if she would be prepared to fly back across the galaxy. The small woman had grinned and replied, *You know me, Carina. I'm not interested in making decisions. I just follow orders.*

No, seriously, Carina had said, *I know it's a big ask. You'll be giving up the chance for a peaceful life planetside.*

But I'm a starship pilot. You think I'm going to have fun ferrying tourists to and from the Bathsheba? *I love that ship, and you're offering me the chance to stay with her forever. Why would I turn you down?*

Carina took Parthenia's hands. "You must continue what you've been doing, building trust between non-mages and mages. And make Letitia one of the family. She's had a hard life growing up as Castiel's daughter."

Her sister bowed her head and tears dripped onto their joined hands. "We could all be dead by the time you come back, if you ever do."

"Then I'll meet your children. They will be beautiful and wonderful, like you."

A great sob burst from Parthenia and she pulled Carina into her arms, weeping on her shoulder. Carina held onto her sister as she cried.

"We've been through so much," Parthenia mumbled.

"And we've grown to know each other so well. I'll never forget you."

For a long time, Parthenia couldn't speak. Eventually, she broke their embrace. "I understand what you must do. It's just that it hurts so much."

"It hurts me too."

Ferne and Oriana were hugging Darius. Nahla hugged Carina, and then suddenly they were all hugging.

"What's going on?"

Bryce had arrived. He was looking at them darkly.

"Carina and Darius are leaving on the *Bathsheba,*" Oriana said, her voice thick. "They're going to find the mages in our sector and tell them about Earth.

He caught Carina's gaze and narrowed his eyes. Then he left.

"Well, now he knows," said Ferne.

THE DAY BEFORE THEIR DEPARTURE, Carina approached Darius. Once they left there would be no turning around, and though her task would be nearly impossible without him, she felt bad about asking him to come with her. She wanted to offer him the option to back out gracefully without hard feelings.

"Darius," she said, "are you sure about this? You're young. You have your whole life ahead of you. You shouldn't have to spend it always helping others."

"Some people are born to a life of service. I was, like you."

"Like me?"

"What else do you think you've been doing all this time except helping mages?"

"I thought I was doing this for myself."

"Really? That doesn't sound like the young merc who rescued a frightened little boy from his kidnappers."

Then she knew he was right.

The Earth authorities were not aware of her plan. Telling them would have created needless complications. There would have been objections, perhaps attempts to prevent them from leaving, but in reality they had no say in the matter.

Too soon, all the tearful reminiscing and promises to stay safe and live happy lives was over. It was time to fly to the *Bathsheba* and begin the final preparations to depart the system. The core of the Black Dogs had boarded the shuttle except for Jackson who, unable to show himself in civilized regions, had already been Transported to the ship. The only new passenger was Alfie Binger. He'd begged to be allowed to join the expedition and Carina had agreed on the proviso he told no one else about it. She couldn't imagine fielding the thousands of Exodus Testifiers who wanted to come along.

Carina was saying her final goodbyes to her siblings, drinking in the sight of them, committing their faces and voices to memory. They'd spent years in close confinement on their starship voyage, too close at times. She knew and loved them inside out. It was not enough, but it would have to be.

She climbed into the shuttle and turned to take a final look at Earth and the people it was breaking her heart to leave.

Someone was riding a bicycle across the landing field. The rider was clearly new to the skill, for the bike swerved and wobbled alarmingly. When he reached the shuttle he leapt from his seat. The bicycle continued on and crashed into the vessel, bounced off it, and fell onto its side, the wheels spinning.

"Carina!" Bryce yelled. "You're really going to leave?" He ran up to her and grabbed her shoulders. "Tell me you weren't going to go without even a word."

"What is there to say? We made it to Earth. You can make a home here now."

"I don't want to make a home on Earth. I came here because I wanted to be with you."

"But I have to leave. I have to go back."

"Then so do I."

She smiled up at him, joy breaking through her sadness. "Let's make the *Bathsheba* our home."

THE END

Thanks for reading Carina's story. I hope you've enjoyed it as much as I enjoyed writing it. If you like science fantasy you might be interested in another series of mine: STAR LEGEND

Sign up to my reader group for a free copy of the *Star Mage Saga* prequel, *Daughter of Discord*, discounts on new releases, review crew invitations and other interesting stuff:

https://jjgreenauthor.com/free-books/

With deepest thanks to patrons

Paul Hanrahan, John Treadwell, Joseph Lau, Peter Samuel Harness, Geeraline Marrs, Bobby Borland, John Stephenson, Chris, William Retsin, Dan Archibald, Grant Ballard-Tremeer Dale Thompson, Jean Gill, Christopher E. Marshall, Cheryl Kuchler, Shan Shwe, Steve Glasper, Donald Swan, Wayne Lampel, Janette S. Mattey, Brian Kelly, Jim, Sarah Woods, Richard L. Adams, Frank Menendez, Patti DeLang, Elizabeth Hickey, Linda Liem, Russ Kirkpatrick, Kate Wilson, Duff Kindt, Catherine Corcoran, Shaun, John Gancz, Dave, Archie Strong, Struggle Session, Susan Cook, Annie Hsiao-Wen Wang, Julian White, Dane Elliot, Iffet a Burton, Gary Johnson, Tracey Paine, Randy Berlin, Ed Cleeves, Amaranth Dawe, Neil, Alex Green, Ann Bryant, Neil Holford

Copyright © 2023 by J.J. Green

All rights reserved.

No part of this book may be reproduced in any form or by any electronic or mechanical means, including information storage and retrieval systems, without written permission from the author, except for the use of brief quotations in a book review.

❀ Created with Vellum

Printed in Great Britain
by Amazon

22474468R00119